THE MOURNING ROSE

MORGAN SMITH

This book is a work of fiction. Nothing in this is remotely based on actual events nor does it take place in any earthbound locale. None of the characters or situations has even a smidgen of reality about them, nor did I write it to get back at my legion of enemies or my arch-nemesis. If you see yourself in one of the characters, you either need a stiff drink, a change in your medication, or a long, hard look in the mirror. This book owes its existence to a lot of people, but most of all to Pat, who always believed.

Cover design and artwork by Steger Productions.

THE MOURNING ROSE

1

The wind was not really that cold as it blew out along the beach, but the men clustered about the two small boats there were shivering, all the same.

"Just when," their leader drawled, "Just when were you planning to advise me of these interestin' facts? Eh, Peterkin? Speak up, man."

Peterkin swallowed, hard. "Well, Jack, I just thought –". He broke off midsentence. It wasn't that Jack looked angry. Indeed, quite the reverse. The dark eyes gazed at him with a kind of sweet benevolence that was more terrifying than any rage might have been.

"You thought? Well done, m'lad. I don't believe I ever asked you to think, of course, although, my memory could well be at fault. I ask you," and here, Jack stopped and looked around, as though appealing for help, "did I ask anyone to think?"

Collectively, they shuffled their feet, mumbling in a negative tone. Of course he hadn't.

In general, when they were alone, they wondered just how it had come to this. How had they come to have Mad Jack as their leader?

It had happened so quickly. They'd heard of him, of course: a wild man, up for any risk, a smuggler other smugglers spoke of with awe, bringing in untold arcane treasures in the darkest of dark nights, laughing in the face of any danger, from armed troops of Excise men to the most horrific of storms – he was a legend in the smuggling world, Mad Jack of the North Beaches was.

And then, suddenly, he was there, in the flesh. Just come to help out old Joe for a few months, and wait for the heat to die down – the Customs Office was onto him, apparently, gotten a wee bit too close for comfort, and why should he not ally himself with them for a time? Brothers in arms, he'd said, comfortably, and Old Joe had fallen in with it, flattered, a bit, that such a famous fellow-traveller would throw in his lot with them.

At first, it had all gone well enough. Mad Jack was respectful, even deferential to Joe, and asked a lot of questions, as if eager to learn from them. And not a bit stingy – he'd stood them to many a mug in the taverns, and once, even, to a slap-up dinner brought in from someplace rather grander than they were used to.

But then, little by little, it had begun to change. There were quiet discussions, where he convinced Old Joe to do things just that little bit differently. There were moments when he'd simply barked out a command, and they had all, unthinkingly, obeyed.

And then that one night, when everything had gone so wrong, when it looked as if every single one of them would have been rounded up and headed for the noose, and only Mad Jack's brazen nerve and quick thinking had saved them. They'd gotten away by the skin of their teeth, because Jack really was mad – mad with no care to his own skin or theirs, and he counted no costs.

They'd had to lie low for a couple of weeks, and when they'd met again, well, those soft words, those words that seemed so kind and reasonable, had convinced them that they had no choice.

It was time that old men took their ease, to live out their days in comfort, Jack said. Time for younger men to take the lead.

Sweet words, all of them, but there was something underneath them that struck terror into even the most stalwart heart. Because there were those other tales - those other stories, the ones about his temper, and about the kind of retribution that seemed to overtake those who crossed him. They had not quite forgotten them, not entirely, and suddenly, they remembered them much too clearly.

So much so that even Joe had looked at his feet and muttered, "Just as you say, Jack," and now sat the watch for them, up at the headlands, and took his share like any of them, and made no sound of discontent.

Because you just never knew what Jack was capable of, did you?

"Well, Peterkin," Jack said, still so sweetly that Peterkin began to tremble, "out with it! A new captain for the Excise men – he has a name, perhaps?"

"Austin, Jack. Captain Austin, was what I think they said. A real fire-eater, they said. Determined to ferret all the smugglers out, root and branch. Coming down from the City in the next seven-day. There's a room bespoke at t' Sun."

Jack closed his eyes.

"Ah," he said. His eyes opened. "Well, let's be moving on, then. Cargo will be waitin', don't you know."

THE SMALLER WITHDRAWING room at Number 4, Shalliton Place, had been given over for the use of the young ladies, and it could not be said that Lady Mayland had spared any expense in furnishing it to provide a most flattering backdrop for her daughter's undeniable beauty. Miss Mayland's fair locks and pale skin were set off admirably by the blue silk wall coverings and the rose velvet settee, so that she looked the very picture of an Imbrian rose. Indeed, several of her most ardent admirers had remarked upon it, and two had actually written poems, likening her to just that flower in its natural garden.

Miss Polyantha Mayland came off rather less well. Her hair, named "auburn" by the more charitable, clashed awkwardly against the pink of the cushions, glinting as it did with strong hints of copper, and her complexion was more vivid and certainly less fashionable than her cousin's. The very walls seemed to rebel against her, as if they would have quelled her brightness if they could.

It was early afternoon, and the pair had only just come in. Their mornings were spent with a Master of the Arts engaged specially to instruct them in the delicate practices of creating suitable Artifices for their future.

No young woman of Fashion could be said to be ready for marriage without such skills. They had formerly been taught by an extremely competent governess, learning the art of turning napkins into snow-white doves that could flutter elegantly down onto a dinner guest's lap. They had mastered the difficult trick of the self-pouring teapots, and both had shown themselves adept at making glowing globes of coloured light float about a midnight garden with apparent ease.

The Master had more exciting spells to impart. His lessons on creating fireworks of dazzling glamour were considerably more taxing than keeping a half-dozen orbs waltzing decorously around the trees, and then there were the "silent footmen" he was teaching them to materialize, in order that no guest would ever lack for even the tiniest courtesy – well, it was all too exhausting to be imagined. Neither young lady had the least assurance that these were skills they could ever command, practice they never so hard.

Still, as Eglantine pointed out, at least they knew how it was done. With luck, they'd marry well enough to hire the Master to do it for them.

"You certainly will," her cousin remarked. "I have no such hopes. If I cannot bring myself to latching onto some poor Scholar at the Academy, I am resolved to remain here in my single state, and be a Prop to my Aunt."

Eglantine gave a whoop of extremely unladylike laughter. "As if she would countenance such a thing! You would quite cut her up if you did, Polly – you know she would dislike it of all things!"

Polyantha managed to retain her expression of martyred inno-cence. "Indeed, she would not! How many times have we heard her sigh over our come-out, and murmur about the passage of time, and how she misses our school-days?"

"Well, but that is only because we are so expensive," said Eglantine, cheerfully. "Once we are safely and eligibly betrothed, she will not care a button for that."

This was undeniably a fact. That very morning, the bill from the milliner's had been in the pile of letters delivered to Lady Mayland at the breakfast table, occasioning some heartfelt sighs and a long discourse on the sacrifices a Mamma must make to ensure her girls would show to advantage in their first Season.

"Not," said Lady Mayland," that I begrudge one copper to outfitting you both, for I do feel as a mother to you, Polly, and would not wish to stint in the least particular. But I must own, it is shocking what these people charge one, considering it is only a square of lace and a scrap of velvet, after all."

Polly had murmured that her Aunt was all kindness, which was quite perfectly true, although it was equally true that the lace and velvet confection had, in fact, been for Lady Mayland herself. Still, considering that Polly was heir to only the merest competence and not likely, given the preference for quiet, well-mannered blondes with large fortunes, to make a particularly brilliant match, her Aunt had always been scrupulously fair in the matter of how she apportioned even the most trivial luxuries between "her girls".

"For you must know," she had often said to her long-suffering husband, "I counted your brother as dear as if he'd been my own, and assured him always that I would treat his daughter as one of the family, which she *is*, Robert! It is a great pity she is so – so *high-spirited*, for I am persuaded that she is the dearest creature otherwise, you know."

"Gracious, look at the time," said Eglantine, suddenly growing less amused. "I declare, those lessons go on and on. Is my hair mussed? You had better ring for tea, Polly. Mrs. Anwing promised faithfully to call today, and bring that new catalogue from Goderets with her. I would not be caught looking less than perfect – you know how she gossips."

"You look adorable," said her cousin, promptly. "Although I don't know why you should care what the Anwing thinks. No one would believe her anyway – not even Lord Valremer."

Eglantine blushed, looking more like an Imbrian rose than ever.

"Eglantine? You are not seriously, that is, you are not thinking –"

Eglantine's cheeks grew even pinker.

"My dearest," Polly began, but broke off as the door opened, and Mrs. Anwing herself appeared, pushing past the footman in a gushing excess of enthusiasm.

Polly, having been enfolded, the next moment, in a brief embrace reeking of some amazingly powerful cologne, retreated to the window seat. Mrs. Anwing's attention was all on Eglantine now. Having clasped her to her bosom as if they had not seen each other for months, she had maneuvered her impeccably-attired and entirely entrancing self onto the settee, and patted the small space remaining beside her invitingly. Dutifully, Eglantine sat down beside her.

In due course, the promised catalogue appeared, and the pair of them began to exclaim over the latest fashions.

It was not, Polly thought, that she was in any way jealous, or even mildly envious of Eglantine's undeniable charms. Lord Valremer might be the most eligible bachelor of this or any other Season, but Polly, having searched her heart, could find nothing that recommended him to her beyond the superficial.

Rich, he most certainly was. Attractive – even handsome – was an undeniable attribute of his. He was not young, of course. He must be all of thirty or more, although Lady Mayland had waved that away with the worldly-wise stricture that it was not uncommon and perhaps even preferable that one's husband be an experienced man of the world.

But there was something about his lordship that unsettled her. He was known as having been, at one time, a singular and admired Practitioner of the Arcane – noted, apparently, when still at school, as being marked for Great Things.

That future had never seemed to materialize. Upon inheriting early (the Valremers were not noted for their longevity) he had embarked on a career of dissipation and debauchery. Not, of course, that Polly was privy to any details, of course – one simply did not discuss such topics with sweetly unmarried and delicately nurtured

Females - but the vague rumours still swirled around his lordship. They had been warned: he had occasionally set up some innocent as his Flirt, and engendered hopes that, alas, would not ever be fulfilled. Those games of his often led to heartache, and, more darkly, it was whispered, occasional ruin.

At first, it seemed that Eglantine had been marked out in much the same way, but she was much too sensible to have taken his overtures as anything but her due as this Season's Non Pareille. Lord Valremer was known to always be at the forefront of fashion – he paid his court to Eglantine along with a hundred other men, as a mere matter of course.

And then something had changed.

The entire City was agog. Had Valremer been caught at last? His behavior had moved from the merely flirtatious to the assiduous. Flowers were sent – not the gaudy bouquets of the ironic lover, but the well-chosen and meaningful posies of a man in earnest. A book of poetry was said to have been sent as well, and that had set tongues wagging in earnest.

And then there were Mrs. Anwing's attentions.

Mrs. Anwing was a widow who had managed, for no adequately explainable reason, to remain at the forefront of Society. She was undeniably lovely, and much admired, at least from a distance. She knew everyone and had gained entrée everywhere, although what, precisely, her social attractions were remained unspoken. Her circumstances were a mystery, too, for while the late Mr. Anwing had certainly not been possessed of enormous wealth, his widow was always dressed in the latest of fashions and kept her own carriage.

She was also possessed of a scathing wit, and perhaps that was how she had maintained such a pre-eminent position. No guest list ever left her name off, and never once had anyone of note failed to acknowledge her when she drove in the Park.

There were some who sought her out over and above the merely courteous, reveling in the latest news that always seemed to come to her ear before anyone else heard a whiff of it.

There were many more, perhaps, who feared her. She was not

above making cruel jests about those who displeased her, and she was quite capable of casting someone into social oblivion, shunned by all, should they happen to incur her wrath: hostesses did not lightly stay friends with the Anwing's victims. Up until now, though, insipid little misses fresh out of the schoolroom had been very much beneath her touch.

Never before had Lord Valremer's third-cousin-by-marriage taken even the slightest notice of any of Valremer's flirtations, save to spread idle gossip about the girl if she lacked for other news. But quite suddenly, she had called at Shalliton Place, graciously leaving her card and an invitation to take tea with her the following week, and after this, to greet all three Mayland ladies with every sign of intimacy and pleasure whenever their paths crossed.

"And I own," Lady Mayland said, when this began, "I do not understand it. She never paid me the slightest heed before, and I wish she would not now. My dear ones, pray, do nothing to upset her!"

As the weeks passed, however, and Lord Valremer's attentions did not withdraw, Mrs. Anwing merely stepped up her efforts. She dropped so many hints that even Lady Mayland began to have some hopes.

Eglantine's mother might continue to caution them both, reminding Eglantine to never be in anything even approaching a compromising situation with Valremer, or anyone else, and to treat his lordship as she would any other undeclared suitor: politely, and with good humour. She might warn them both not to permit any man even the tiniest intimacy, but these strictures were almost afterthoughts, sandwiched between speculations on how much the Valremer fortune actually was, and whether or not Eglantine would prefer to spend her days at Valremer Court down in Summersett, or preside over the staff at Orpington Circle.

Polly kept her own counsel, for once. She, too, was dumbfounded by Valremer's continued interest: it seemed absurd. Eglantine was certainly the most lovely girl to have made her curtsey this Season, and she was as good-tempered and generous of spirit as she was pretty. She managed her would-be admirers with sweetness and tact, never allowing any of them to feel slighted, and she had, moreover, the Mayland pedigree. Not a single family in the City could have found the slightest fault with Miss Mayland as their son's chosen bride.

But Valremer had seemed to be a confirmed non-starter in the marriage stakes. No less than twenty such girls must have swept through their Season with just as much to recommend them, and he had not fallen. Polly adored her cousin, but even so, in her heart of hearts, she could not see that there was anything so much different about Eglantine than those unknown others Valremer had passed by.

It made no sense at all.

2

Her Grace, the Dowager Duchess of Ambridge, had just finished dressing for dinner, and was settling herself at her escritoire to look over her correspondence when her son, the current Duke, strolled in.

"Jarod!" she said, with real pleasure, and then stopped, a little dismayed.

His Grace was dressed in evening wear of the very latest style. His black trousers sported some very fine silk braid along the seams, his black satin waistcoat was delicately patterned in a style reminiscent of the Oriental, and his black frock coat was so exquisitely fitted that one scarcely needed to imagine the muscles beneath.

It was not his attire which upset her, although she did, in the back of her mind, reflect that her son paid entirely too much and too fastidious an attention to his wardrobe and appearance, far more than any man she'd ever known, and far too much for a young man who had, until recently, been an officer in the Army, and used to living rough.

But it was his face that concerned her. He looked heavy-eyed, as if he had gone some time without sleep, and his mouth, usually so ready to laugh, was grim.

"Jarod," she repeated. "Do not tell me you have only just come in!"

The grimness vanished, replaced by a mischievous grin. He raised an eyebrow. "Do not ask me, then, dearest!"

He moved gracefully across the room to take her outstretched hand to drop a careless kiss on her wrist, and then he recoiled.

"What the devil kind of scent are you wearing, Mother?"

Her face fell.

"It is 'Eau d'Ilrae'," she said. "It is all the rage, so Hermina says, and you know how she follows the fashions. I made sure you would like it excessively!"

"Well, I do not," her son said, forcefully. "You aren't meant for such things. You want something floral, Mother. I've told you so a hundred times. Sweets for the sweet, my dear."

"Well, I did think it was a little odd," she confessed. "But Hermina was so sure...Jarod, you have turned the conversation nicely, but still! Were you out all night?"

"Not all of it," he said, smiling. "Just the best part. Come, Mother, admit it. You would hate it if I hung about the house and interfered with you having things just as you like them."

"Well," she said, "perhaps not quite that. But I hardly see you, these days. Not since – not –" but here she faltered, and her eyes filled with tears.

"Not since Adrian's funeral," said her son, harshly. "I know, Mother. I know. I'm a poor replacement, as a son and as a Duke. But we must get on as best we can."

"That isn't what I meant," she cried. "I loved you both! And I know you mean to do right by your position, and I have every confidence in you. It is only that..."

There was a silence. She could hear the faint ticking of the great casement clock in the hall outside.

"I miss him, too," said Jarod, softly.

～

POLLY HAD ALWAYS, even before her coming-out, wondered at the languid air of ennui that so many girls seemed to adopt. The balls, the concerts, the picnics and outings that were forever being arranged for the sole amusement of young people still seemed like an enchantment to her.

She was quite aware that these entertainments had a dual purpose, in that they were organized to throw eligible parties together in hopes of the appropriate attachments being formed, but that knowledge had not lessened her enjoyment. What did it matter, after all, since they afforded her pleasure? If the young men did not flock to her side in such great numbers as they did to Eglantine's, she still had her admirers, and not all of them were second sons or Scholars living on tiny stipends from the Academy. If not accounted a beauty, she was still said to be "very handsome", her lively commentary on the quirks of the world was considered witty and brave, and she had, in fact, already received one serious proposal.

Not that she was supposed to know about that. Lady Mayland might consider a titled gentleman of over thirty suitable husband material for a Reigning Toast, but Lord Mayland was not disposed to sell off his niece to a Professor of The Arts who was well past fifty and had two adult children, besides. Polly might not bring great wealth to the man she married, but she was a Mayland, after all, and that, in her uncle's eyes, was worth a great deal more than mere money.

Still, Lady Mayland's grasp on discretion was not firm, and a few things had slipped out. Between these, an unannounced interview between the Professor and Lord Mayland at an unfashionably early hour, and the sudden departure of said Professor from the City to his sister's home in the North, Polly had determined the truth of the matter.

She was at once relieved and affronted. Relieved because she knew herself to be tenderhearted, and could well have imagined herself acquiescing so as not to hurt the old man's feelings, and affronted, because, well, it seemed rather high-handed not to even be consulted about it.

Relief won out, however. She saw that her uncle had merely

wished to spare her any discomfort, and it was, as she pointed out to Eglantine, rather flattering that Uncle thought she could do much better. She thought he was mistaken, but it was kind of him to think so.

"Goose," said Eglantine, fondly. "Any man would be lucky to marry you. They all adore you. Every one of them clamors to dance with you and escort you to supper, and hand you into the carriage. Many another girl cannot say so much."

"That's because they are hoping I will sing their praises to you, dearest. Besides, they must do something, while waiting for you to notice them!"

Eglantine shook her head.

"What about the young duke? The one who died? He didn't have but two words for Mamma or me, but he stood up with you twice at the Paltravers' ball. And he plucked that rose for you from the archway – that was remarked upon by everyone: such a pretty gesture! Mamma said he watched you the rest of the night as if he could not bear to let you out of his sight!"

"Ambridge? Poor man. It was a shocking thing, was it not? But truthfully, Eglantine, it was just the one evening. Chances are, if he had lived, he would not even have noticed me again. Or decided, however engaging, that your poor relation was not up to snuff."

"Perhaps." Eglantine sounded doubtful. "He seemed very much struck, though. Mamma was so pleased. She said he looked a man in love if ever there was."

Polly shook her head. "We hardly spoke. How could we know if we would suit? It was one ball, Eglantine. You can't call that love."

ACROSS TOWN, Mrs. Anwing was dressing carefully for the evening ahead. She had a most beautiful gown of puce satin, trimmed with soft, cobwebby lace imported all the way from Evannion and dyed to match the satin exactly. At each dip of the trim's scallop, there was a tiny chip of charmed, faceted glass, so that every movement she made caused a ripple of magenta sparkle to glisten around her. It was the height of fashion, and not for the first time, she gave silent, if slightly resentful, thanks to her cousin, who made such things possible. The long-departed Mr. Anwing had certainly not been in a position to have dressed her like this.

This was, she reminded herself, a night that would bring her closer to freedom, to even greater things. All she had to do was to play her part, and she need never worry over a dressmaker's bill again. A few more weeks, perhaps, if nothing went wrong. She was determined that this time, nothing would.

Not like before, she had said to him, greatly daring.

He had not quite agreed with her, but she saw that he was being more careful. He had rushed it, before, and look how that had turned out. Weeks of work, with so much energy poured into the thing, and all for naught.

She had tried to warn him, she had known it wouldn't serve, but it had done no good.

Men, she thought, scornfully. They were always so quick to dismiss a woman's counsel, and look where it got them.

The door of her boudoir opened and she gave a guilty start, smoothing the discontented look from her face as she turned. It would never do to let him see even the tiniest spark of defiance. He had a temper, underneath that lazy smile, and she had seen what he could do, when he thought himself thwarted.

She shivered, despite herself, but it was only her maid, bringing her a gauze shawl against the non-existent evening chill.

CAPTAIN AUSTIN WAS ENJOYING his last days in the City as best he could. He had eaten a well-grilled chop at his sister's house, washing it down with a superb claret, and had followed this up with a look-in at a gaming house he was fond of. Seeing no one he knew, he then sauntered down to Wilde's, where he was certain to find congenial company and a game of Hazard, and had managed to while away three hours most pleasantly before looking up to meet a pair of eyes he was considerably less than happy to encounter.

At the unspoken words, he made some jesting excuse and left the table, heading for the small library at the back of the club.

Moments later, he was joined by an exquisite in full evening dress of the utmost style and cut.

"I didn't expect to see you here, my lord," he said.

"Why ever not, Lionel? I am a member still, I trust? Carruthers seemed to think so, when he took my hat."

"Don't be – that is, I only meant – well, it's scarcely two months since –," he broke off. The cold look in his companion's eyes told him this was not a subject worth pursuing.

"Let us skip the idle pleasantries," said the man. "What can you tell me about this season's plans for thwarting the smugglers of Summersett?"

"Sir," protested the captain. "You know that I cannot possibly –"

There was a lightning flash of steel, and the captain found there was a knife pressed suddenly against his throat.

"I beg to differ," said his companion, pleasantly. "Indeed, I think it more than possible. I think it entirely probable...and wise, too. Do you not agree?"

Captain Austin made a small sound of submission.

THE ASSEMBLY ROOMS were almost unbearably hot, despite every window having been opened to admit the faint autumn breeze. Lady Mayland fanned herself vigorously as she scanned the room, noting approvingly that her niece was dancing with Captain Ryssington, of whom she had the highest hopes. He had originally formed part of Eglantine's court, and that had fretted her mother somewhat, since Eglantine had seemed to find more than ordinary pleasure in his company. Lately, however, Lady Mayland fancied his attentions to dear Polly had seemed to have grown into something more than a wish to ingratiate himself as a stepping-stone towards the Reigning Toast.

He was not especially wealthy, but he was spoken of as a promising officer, sure to make his mark in military circles. And in his Home Guards uniform, he was so very dashing! Even the Anwing had remarked upon it.

Lady Mayland would have been quite disappointed to discover that Theodore Ryssington, in a most un-lover-like fashion, was attempting to lecture Polly on her interest in a recent bout of fisticuffs that she should not, in his opinion, have even the faintest knowledge of.

"Dash it, Polly, it ain't what a respectable female is supposed to talk about!"

His efforts were hampered by the movements of the dance, which at that exact moment took Polly out of his orbit as she linked arms with the gentleman beside her and was whisked away in a promenade down the line.

He had, perforce, to take the arm of another lady and respond politely to her remarks about the unseasonable heat, and when he found himself with Polly again, he had rather lost his train of thought.

The dance ended. Captain Ryssington regrouped and began to again explain to Polly just why she should not inquire too closely into the workings of the magickal charm Major Everard had used to teach young Listral a lesson in the ring, when she stopped suddenly in mid-step, and her hand dropped away from his arm.

He turned. She was looking quite shocked, and her eyes were now focused on the upper end of the room, in a very peculiar way.

"The deuce –," Ryssington began to say, and then stopped. He looked in the direction she was peering towards, but saw nothing whatever out of the ordinary.

"Are you all right, Polly?"

She blinked, shaking her head. "I thought – I thought I saw...but no. It isn't possible." She looked at him, and despite her agitation, smiled weakly. "I am so sorry, Theo. Indeed, I am perfectly well. I just thought I saw – well, no matter. The merest nothing. Now, what were you saying about Major Everard?"

ON THE OTHER side of the room, Mrs. Anwing was working herself into a state.

Where, in the name of every demon of the Nine Hells, was Valremer?

She watched as Eglantine, adorably attired in a gown of the palest blue, embroidered with tiny silver stars that winked fetchingly in the candlelight, stepped out onto the floor on the arm of Mr. Wisley, with every evidence of being perfectly pleased to be dancing with him.

Drat her cousin. Had he changed his mind about the timing, and not thought it worth telling her? She was half-minded to give him a set-down, she thought, but even as she considered the words she might use to disabuse him of the notion that she was not integral to his schemes and needed to be kept abreast of his plans, her heart sank.

She would not ever say the words. She didn't dare so much as think them when in his presence, and not merely because she would then have to find the means to pay her dressmaker herself.

3

The common room of the Golden Sun Hostelry was as crowded as it had ever been, owing to the rumour of a Prize Match between two hedge-mages of considerable repute. The rough-tongued and woolen-clad locals rubbed shoulders with Blades of the Blood, sharing the high spirits that such sports always occasion. The fashionable men who had descended on the little port town of Summerpoole were in fine fettle and generous moods, frequently calling for rounds for their rustic comrades, while making bets on the outcome of the match that would, hopefully, commence on the morrow.

Old Joe's dark and somber countenance sat poorly with his fellows. From time to time, those who knew him made attempts to pull him out of the sullens, to no avail. His mug of ale had been sitting before him, untouched, for nearly an hour, and every time the door opened, he would start, looking over at the newcomer with a mixture of disappointment and relief.

He began to seem more comfortable, as the second hour waxed and waned, and whoever he had been expecting failed to materialize. He took a pull of his drink, and stretched a little, seeming to finally relax.

This was only a short-lived reprieve, he discovered. The landlord's son made his way through the crowd of roisterers and leaned down to shout into Old Joe's ear.

"Da says you're to go on into t' parlour."

Joe looked around, apprehensively.

"Did he say wh--?" It was too late. Tompkin was already moving away, pushing past a boy in a Guards' uniform and young Sammy Horner, who were arm-in-arm and dancing something that vaguely resembled a jig.

He rose and made his reluctant way to the farther door, and slipped out into the narrow hall. The parlour door was just on the latch and a faint sliver of light was peeping through. Old Joe pushed it open and stepped over the threshold.

There was a bottle of claret, already open and waiting on the table beside the one lone candle.

Joe wasn't much for wine – he thought it a thin and sour thing, and disappointing, most times – but he needed some courage, just then. He poured himself a half a glass, and sat down in one of two chairs drawn up there, huddling into the small circle of light, and trying to settle his nerves with a healthy swig.

He didn't have to wait for long, looking up as the man strolled into the room, bold as brass, and dressed in what most people in Summerpoole would have called "flash". How did the gentry even move in those close-fitting garments? He had often wondered about it, but then, the gentry didn't have to do too much, when all was said and done.

"Well, then," said his visitor. "Pour me some of that wine, since I've paid for it, and tell me the news."

Joe concentrated on filling a second glass.

"It's been quiet, yer lordship. Very quiet. And the weather's been against us, you might say. Windy. Very windy."

"Really? I hadn't heard that." There was a note in the man's voice that made Joe a mite nervous, but he had an answer ready for this.

"Well, it don't affect shipments from the west. Those winds is the same as ever. But I heard that there's been powerful great storms away south. Said to be very dangerous, those are."

"I see."

"Will ye be sendin' the young lord back to collect the booty when it comes in, yer lordship? Because I have to say –"

"No!" This time, the man's voice cracked like a whip. "No," he repeated. "I will come myself. You need only send word."

The room fell silent. Joe could hear the muffled sound of merriment from the common room, all laughter, cheers and bawdy songs, and he wished, not for the first time, that he had never been drawn into these waters.

"It might be tricky," he said, after a bit. "There's a new captain of the Excise coming down to take charge, or so they say. A real goer, determined to put an end to the trade, or so they reckon. Some of the lads, well, they don't like it, sir. "

"What do their likes or dislikes have to do with it? Are you not their leader?"

Joe picked up his glass and appeared to be searching for his answers there. "Aye," he said, after a moment. "Aye, I'm the leader, right enough. They'll do their part. But if this new man's all they say he is, well, we might run into difficulties, that's all."

The man's lip curled. "You may safely disregard the captain. I assure you, he will not trouble you. Only do your part and bring me my shipment. Surely this task is not beyond you?"

"Er – no, no. We can do it, right enough. You say I should just send word? To the usual place?"

"Just so. " The man rose. "You'll be desolated, I know, but I have a pressing engagement in town. One must never disappoint a lady."

With that, he was gone, leaving an exhausted but much relieved Joe to contemplate the gentleman's probable means of locomotion, since Summerpoole was a full thirty miles from the City, and to hope, very much, that he had managed this meeting as he'd been instructed to.

IT WAS the custom of the Assembly to shut the doors firmly against the tardy, once the last of the Late Evening Bells had sounded.

Lord Valremer crossed that august threshold just as the final peal was echoing in the street, but even had he been a little slower, it is doubtful the two footmen, whose duty it was to bar any latecomers, would have denied him. His lordship was known to be short-tempered, and any threats of job loss would have been outweighed by their very real nervousness at what sort of retaliation he might have brought down, had they adhered more strictly to their instructions.

Mrs. Anwing, catching sight of him at once, managed to disengage herself adroitly from a tedious conversation with the aging Marquess of Gallarym, and moved to intercept her cousin on a route that would have taken him not to Eglantine's side, but to the smaller card room. She pushed past a man in a black satin waistcoat, who was bending down to pick up a young lady's gilt fan from the floor.

"What have you been playing at?" she hissed, furiously, as she came up to Valremer's side. "The girl's stood up with young Calthorpe twice already. Did we not agree on a strategy?"

"Calm yourself, cousin," he said. He sounded amused. "I know better than you how to reel in this fish."

"Do you?" she asked, goaded. "Do you, indeed, my lord? She seems mighty unaffected by your absence."

It was true. Eglantine looked perfectly content, surrounded by a full dozen admirers, content and not in the least as if she noticed any defectors. But then, as if compelled by some arcane force, she looked up and towards the pillared entranceway where Valremer stood, and Mrs. Anwing saw the tiny but unmistakable change in the girl, even from this distance. Relief? Or simply gladness? Mrs. Anwing did not know, but she did not care. Valremer would do the thing, and this time, Powers willing, he would not fail at the last fence.

"Our cue, I think," said her cousin, indifferently. "Do try to look less in a pet, Merelia. It is a happy occasion, is it not?"

They stepped away from the pillars. Behind them, the man in the black satin waistcoat took up their now-vacated place. It was, in fact, the perfect spot for surveying everything in the room.

$\backsim$

IT HAD BEEN, Polly thought, an utterly enchanting evening. She had danced nearly every dance, because Andrew Calthorpe, Theo, and their brother officers considered her in the light of their social mascot: she was not the least put out by being used as a way to remain close to this season's Beauty without looking hangdog or obvious, and she was not at all missish or a prude. A Good Sport, Andrew had said, and no one disagreed.

The music was delightful, the conversation amusing, and the glass of orgeat someone brought her during the Short Interval had been just how she liked it. In fact, despite that one moment of confusion – surely her eyes had been playing tricks on her! – it had been, to her mind, exactly the kind of evening a girl's first Season should consist of.

A shadow now fell over these thoughts. She had looked up just at the same moment as Eglantine had, and it was rather as if the candles had dimmed of their own free will.

Valremer, having arrived to greet Lady Mayland with easy courtesy, turned and moved past the young men who crowded around Eglantine. Indeed, they might as well have been elsewhere, so little did their existence trouble him.

"My lord," Eglantine said, in a chaffing tone, "I swear I gave you up hours ago. It is too bad, for you asked for the Quadrille, and had not Mr. Wisley taken pity on me, I should have had to sit it out."

Valremer possessed himself of her hand, which, despite her mock scolding, she had held out to him.

"You will forgive me, my goddess, I hope. Only the most pressing business could have kept me from you side, did you but know it. And there are still more dances."

He bent and kissed her wrist.

"Forgiveness you may have," Eglantine said, "but there are only three dances remaining, and I am afraid they are all promised, my lord."

"I am properly punished for my sins, then, am I not?"

She laughed. "You may take it that way, if you like. Lieutenant Calthorpe, I believe the couples are forming up. Shall we not join them?"

Polly watched as Andrew moved with eagerness to Eglantine's side. Valremer gave way with grace, and watched them go.

No one was looking at him, of course. They were all watching Eglantine, who glided into place on Andrew's arm as if she were floating. She had never looked lovelier, thought Polly, and stole a glance at her cousin's erstwhile swain.

Like the others, his eyes were on Eglantine. And he knew that, perhaps. He knew that for this one moment, he was unobserved, and perhaps he let his guard down, just a little.

For a brief instant, Valremer's expression was not that of a man in love. It was not even the look of a man appreciating beauty as it materialized before him.

He looked, Polly thought, in sudden confusion, like a wolf who has cornered his prey.

Behind her, she heard the sound of lace tearing and a squawk of ill-tempered distress.

"Powers!" Mrs. Anwing said, much annoyed. "Clumsy oaf! Just look at my gown."

Polly turned.

"But what has happened, ma'am?" she asked.

Mrs. Anwing was holding up her skirts just a little, inspecting the damage.

"That idiot – over there. Trod right on my hem. Just look – it is all torn!" She was not exaggerating. A full five inches of delicately webbed scallop was hanging forlornly from the edge of the satin gown. Polly looked down the hall, and then shrugged. It was impossible to say which of the gentlemen milling about the terrace doors the Anwing was referring to.

"And he did not even have the grace to stop and apologize."

"Indeed, it is too bad," Lady Mayland agreed. "Polly, dearest, have you any Invisible Menders? Do accompany Mrs. Anwing to the cloakroom and help her. "

Polly nodded. She always had mending charms in her reticule, since torn hems were a constant trial to her cousin. Some of the gentlemen were so enthralled with Eglantine's countenance that they quite forgot where their feet were.

"It is no matter," said Mrs. Anwing, suddenly abandoning her pique. "I daresay my maid can fix it. I would not trouble you for the world, Polly. Are you not engaged for the next dance?"

"No, no, you cannot mean it." Lady Mayland protested. "Such lovely lace. Did you have it from Honorine's? If you leave it, it might be ruined beyond repair! Indeed, Mrs. Anwing, you must mend it instantly! There is plenty of time. Polly can manage it in a trice -I expect you will be back before the second promenade."

"There is always such a crush, though. I wouldn't for the world discommode the young people, just for a silly dress."

"Mr. Wisley will not mind, just this once, I am certain. You do see the urgency, do you not, Mr. Wisley?"

This was an open question. Mr. Wisley tore his eyes away from Eglantine taking a courtesy corner with Lieutenant Calthorpe, looked uncomprehendingly at the lace and satin in question, and muttered, "Just so, Lady Mayland."

"There," said Polly's aunt, comfortably. "It is all settled."

Mrs. Anwing's prediction proved all too correct, however. It took the pair of them an age to navigate the crowds blocking the steps leading down to the Ladies' Cloakroom, and by the time they had gained the relative calm of that place, the unfortunate lady's irritation had returned. She snapped impatiently at the attendant who tried to assist them in the repairs, and grumbled crossly about idle loiterers who came to an Assembly merely to quiz everyone who walked by.

The next set had already formed by the time Polly regained the ballroom. Somewhere in the return journey, she had completely lost Mrs. Anwing in the throng, but a well-known widow of eight-and-twenty needed no constant chaperone, and Polly was rather relieved not to have to listen to another diatribe regarding clumsy, ill-mannered men who could not mind their feet.

She came back to aunt's side, only a little annoyed with having missed the Sarabande. Mr. Wisley, unsurprisingly, was dancing with his sister, Belinda.

It was, if anything, even hotter in the ballroom than it had been before. The terrace doors might be flung wide, but very little of the breeze was reaching the upper end of the room. She groped for her fan.

"My love, do you see Eglantine? I believe she had promised this dance to Lord Huntingfield."

Polly scanned the dancers, and then frowned.

"Are you sure? I don't see Freddie, either."

Lady Mayland said doubtfully, "I made sure she said she was standing up with Huntingfield."

She patted her aunt's hand. "Perhaps she was too hot, and they have gone for some small refreshment," she said. "Depend on it: she cannot have gone far."

The dance was ending. Lord Mayland emerged from the small card room, Huntingfield at his side, and it appeared they were having some small discussion, and not one that the younger man seemed entirely happy with.

"I tell you, sir," Huntingfield was saying as they reached Lady Mayland's side, "The message was quite clear. I mistook nothing – the man said you desired me to wait upon you in the card room."

"Curious," said Mayland, with the air of a man who was now barely hanging onto his patience. "Yet I must tell you again, I asked no one to give you any such message. Depend on it, if you heard aright, then it is this servant who has garbled the thing or some such. I hope no one may be discommoded by it."

"Oh dear," Polly said. "Eglantine is not with you, Lord Huntingfield?"

"I – er, no. Dash it, that's what I'm saying. I was meant to stand up with her, but then this man came and desired me to come into the card room."

"And you just left her there?" Polly was scornful. "Upon my word, Freddie, that is not very pretty conduct!"

Lord Huntingfield quailed. "No, no. That is, I mean, Valremer was nearby. He said he would be delighted to dance with her, and – dash it all, Polly, she was perfectly happy for him to do so."

This last bit, uttered in a rather depressed tone, silenced her, but it had the opposite effect on her aunt. Having listened in a slightly bewildered, worried fashion to these comments, she now lost her fretfulness and said, "Very handsome of him, I'm sure. But then, he is always so kind to our dear girl. Depend on it, he will have taken every care of her."

"But where are they, ma'am?" asked Polly. "Dance with her he most certainly did not. I could not see either of them among the couples, and Lord Valremer, at least, is not easy to lose in a crowd."

"It will be as you said." Lady Mayland sounded confident. "They will have stepped into the supper-room to take some orgeat against the heat."

There was a pause. The couples would be forming for the final set very soon. Polly looked at the crestfallen expression on Lord Hunt-ingfield's face, and took pity on him.

"Freddie, you could go and make sure of them, could you not? After all, she promised this dance to Mr. Ryssington, and if she has not noticed the time...It would be the greatest kindness to us if you would."

He accepted the commission with alacrity, glad to be out from under the increasing glower of Lord Mayland, who was now thor-oughly annoyed with both his daughter and her collective suitors. But even as he began to make his way towards the lower end of the ballroom, Polly caught sight of her cousin.

They were just coming through the terrace doors, Eglantine leaning on Valremer's arm, but before anyone, near or far, could register this apparent breach of maidenly modesty, Mrs. Anwing appeared behind them, looking sleekly pleased and proprietorial.

Eglantine's cheeks were flushed and she seemed almost faint as the trio made their way past the dancers congregating at the centre of the ballroom.

Valremer – Polly could not read his expression. It might have been triumph. Certainly he was not displeased. Her heart gave an almost imperceptible lurch. Something about this seemed odd.

"Eglantine! My love, you had us quite worried," Lady Mayland seemed to have finally caught a little of her husband's mood. "But of course, with Mrs. Anwing – my dear, you are very good to have accompanied her, I do thank you – naturally, I need have no worries."

Polly looked at her cousin, still gripping Valremer's arm.

"Are you quite well, Eglantine?"

"Oh! Oh, yes. That is, I was a little – a little lightheaded – the heat, you know! That is why we went out onto the terrace. For the breeze."

But she was not looking at Polly. Her eyes were cast down, fixed on the tips of her dancing slippers peeking out from under the swirls of pale blue muslin, and as the hectic flush receded from her cheeks, it occurred to Polly that her cousin looked unnaturally pale.

4

I t had been a relief, at the end of the evening, to step out of the doors into the cooler night air, and to stand under the portico while they waited for their carriage. The steps were crowded, and in that crush, they had rather lost sight of some of their friends, Valremer included.

A pity, said Lady Mayland. Indeed, did not Lord Mayland think so? For she was sure, the way he looked at them – and here, for a mercy, she lowered her voice – that he had been on the point of asking Lord Mayland for An Interview.

Lord Mayland ignored this, and took out his snuffbox.

Captain Ryssington worked his way past a group of young men who were considering a wager on whose carriage would appear first.

"Look here, Polly," he said. "I've got to get the little Alton back to barracks. He's quite foxed, and I can't leave him on his own. But you will think on what I said, won't you?"

Before she could reply, he was gone.

"You see?" said Eglantine. "Not just poor Ambridge, Polly."

"Indeed?" They hadn't seen Mrs. Anwing come up. "I didn't know you had been acquainted with his Grace, Polly."

"I was not, I assure you," Polly said. "And Theo did not intend that as it sounded, Eglantine. You know he did not."

"Then, what did you mean, Miss Mayland, about poor Ambridge?"

"Oh," said Eglantine, "it was the most romantic thing. And so sad, too, in the end. The Duke saw Polly at a ball, and was instantly smitten. But then..." her voice trailed off.

The carriage arrived. They said their good-byes and were handed into their seats. The carriage-door was shut, and they were suddenly, and for Polly, mercifully, in darkness and quiet.

The shades were drawn, and so none of them noticed as the man in the black satin waistcoat emerged from the shadows of the portico to stand watching the Mayland coach, rumbling down the street.

ALONE IN HER ROOM, the second parlourmaid who "did" for her having gone, at long last, to her own bed, Polly had lain awake, still troubled by too many disconnected and worrisome thoughts to sleep.

Finally, she sat up, lit her bedside candle, and then took it with her over to the carved armoire in the corner. She opened the doors, and unfastened the latch on the little drawer at its base. Underneath her embroidered shawl from Meresia, and her best kid gloves, lay the small casket containing her few treasures: her mother's pearl set in a velvet-covered case, her gilt-and-turquoise hair combs, three elegant gold bangles, and the pair of diamond ear-bobs Lord Mayland had given her on her sixteenth birthday.

And the much-acclaimed and much-admired book of poetry her father had written.

She pulled out the volume, smoothing her fingers over the tooled leather cover. On the fly-leaf, she knew, were those familiar words of love, a man's dedication of ardent sentiments to the lady who had won his heart, and then, added later in a different ink, his adoration for a newborn daughter.

She did not, when she finally opened the book, spare even a

glance at those heartfelt sentiments, but flipped past to the third set of verses.

> *The dance we danced was more than dance,*
> *A measure perfect as the moon;*
> *Now bereft am I in summer's sunlight;*
> *For that you shall not return so soon.*

THERE, on the page opposite, lay a rose.

It had been, when gifted, of a purest, most delicate cream colour, tinged at the edges of those fragrant petals with the deepest, truest pink. A symbol of virtue, of springtime, of beginnings.

It was with no little horror that she looked at the rose now.

It ought, in the normal course of events, to have withered somewhat. That fleshy bloom ought to have faded, and the blush of its coral extremities ought to have become browned with the weeks of lightless impressment. It ought to have been as flat and as dead a thing as its donor.

It was not.

It sprang out from the vellum leaves like a kitten in pursuit of a ball of yarn, as if it had been laid there not two minutes before, and it gave off, once more, that familiar, ghostly scent of a night long past.

But that was the least of it.

For what had once been a perfect, virginal, Imbrian rose was now ashen-grey, and its edges had turned completely black.

And in the air around her, she sensed a rustling, whispering sound, faint at first, but with a gathering force.

"Remember me and hold me close...for a little while..."

~

"A LITTLE HIGHER," said Master Sempervirens, somewhat testily. "A little higher, please, Miss Polyantha. The point is to entertain your guests with beauty, not have it blind them by exploding the Works in their faces."

Polly sighed. She was more than ordinarily inept at creating her fireworks this afternoon, and the Master, not having Eglantine's presence to dazzle and distract him, was far less forgiving of her blunders.

The day had not begun well. It was overcast, yet still unbearably hot, and although there had been a brief drizzle during the night, it merely succeeded in making the morning more humid, and therefore more ennervating still.

Eglantine had slept unusually late. When she finally arose, her countenance was so waxen, and her movements so languid that her mother had immediately ordered her back to bed, fretting about fevers and worrying aloud that her condition might prevent their appearance at the Opera that evening. Since the box had been rented at considerable expense, and new gowns purchased as well, this would obviously be a disaster. Eglantine, framed by the opulent draperies and looking her very best was, in Lady Mayland's opinion, the very thing needed to bring a hesitant suitor to the sticking-point.

And thus Polly was now enduring the sole attentions of Master Sempervirens. Robbed of the aesthetic pleasure of Eglantine's beauty, his impatience with her cousin's lack of talent had surfaced in the form of one or two rather waspish remarks, and a distinct lack of deference.

She succeeded, on her fifth attempt, in setting off a small burst of showering sparks in a vaguely floral arrangement, at a height that might not actually set anyone on fire, at which point Master Sempervirens muttered that it was an improvement of sorts and ended the lesson well short of the two hours normally allotted.

He took his leave with the heartfelt hope that Miss Mayland would soon be on her feet once more, but Polly did not at once return to the house. She walked, instead, to the long end of the garden and finding that the bench under the row of alder trees was relatively dry, sat down and tried to sort out her thoughts.

On further consideration, she realized that Valremer could not have done other than as he had. Finding Eglantine near to swooning in the heat, what could have been more natural than to escort her somewhere cooler? And not unchaperoned, since Mrs. Anwing had been by their side, so there could not be the least impropriety about moving onto the terrace.

A stray and evanescent though drifted to her, that Mrs. Anwing had not always been at Eglantine's side, but she brushed it away. She could not, at this point, be sure that this was so, since it had taken her some few minutes to work her way back to Lady Mayland's side, and she was not perfectly certain just when Valremer had persuaded Eglantine to leave the ballroom. It might easily have been after Mrs. Anwing had joined them. Indeed, knowing Eglantine's good sense in social matters, she must believe that this was the case, and that her cousin had had no notion of being alone with any gentleman, no matter how persuasive and polished his addresses, nor how wearying the heat might have been.

She put a hand to her brow, as if to ease the pressure of her tumbling thoughts, for the odd behavior of Eglantine when the trio had returned to her aunt's side was not even half of her worries.

The strangeness of what had occurred when she was alone in her room still consumed her. She had shoved the book back into the drawer and slammed the armoire shut, leaping back into her bed so precipitately that she had not even stopped to blow out her little candle – it had guttered out sometime after she had at last fallen into a fitful sleep.

What had possessed her to look at that rose, after so long?

She had not thought more than errantly about his Grace, Duke of Ambridge, for weeks. No one had mentioned his name to her until that afternoon. The world, it seemed, had been content to forget him, once he had been decently buried and his brother invested with his former honours. It had been an unpleasant shock, a young man dying so suddenly, and in such dubious circumstances. It made people uncomfortable; they had not liked to think on it, and Polly, too, had buried her own thoughts of that handsome face and the wry, almost sad, smile that had graced it as it he offered her the rose.

It must have been her imagination. It must have been, for there was no other explanation for that rushing roar of whispering wind past her ears. Her imagination, and a trick of the light, that had turned the pale bloom into a ghostly lamentation.

EGLANTINE HAD QUITE RECOVERED her spirits and her complexion by the time the afternoon tea tray was brought in. She sat on the rose velvet settee, a book of fashion plates on her lap, trying to decide if she preferred the bonnet of starched Gallican lace or the rather more jaunty cap modeled after the Home Guards' summer shako, and she firmly declared her intention to drive out with Polly to Mademoiselle Collette's Emporium, to look at hair ribbons.

"Such a dismal day, Mamma. We shall be teased into fits if we do not find *something* to amuse us!"

Lady Mayland, relieved at her daughter's swift recovery, was inclined to agree.

"Do but remember to look for something in a dark lavender, my loves. I had a card from Lady Sackler just this morning. A little evening concert, you know, very quiet and select, and she writes that Her Grace of Ambridge may attend. She is still in mourning, of course, poor soul, and one *utterly* would not wish to offend, so it shall have to be the purple satin – why, Polly, dearest, whatever is the matter?"

"Nothing – I – oh, Aunt, I am sorry!"

Polly, white-faced, gazed at the ruins of the tea cup, lying on the silver tray where it had fallen from her suddenly nerveless fingers.

"No matter, my love," Lady Mayland said, promptly. "I have never really liked this set of tea things. They were a wedding-gift from Cousin Albertine - so terribly old-fashioned and dreary, are they not? And heavy, too; it is most fatiguing. I must ask Lord Mayland if we might not have a new set, in the southern style. They are all the rage, you know. Eglantine, if you are driving out with Polly, you had better wear your old half-boots. It looks as if it may rain again, and I would not for the world have you ruin your new ones."

A fine thing, Polly thought irritably, as she and Eglantine climbed into the landaulet, when the very mention of an Ambridge could drive her instantly witless. And why, she wondered, after two months of silence, was everyone suddenly determined to talk so endlessly about the dead Duke and his family?

She had meant, when Eglantine suggested this outing, to have asked her cousin about last night. She had only wanted to make sure that Eglantine had not been coaxed by some means into doing something unwise, to see if Valremer's interest was as engaged as Lady Mayland supposed, or if this was not, in the end, some flirtation gone too far.

But the mention of the Dowager Duchess, coming on the heels of that terrifying moment the night before, drove those concerns deeply underground, and later, having ransacked Madame Collette's pyramids of satin ribbons and embroidered silk wraps, and then climbed back into the conveyance, she found that Eglantine was not disposed to discuss it at all. Either by happenstance or design, the conversation remained centred on the many invitations and amusements still to come, and Polly, perhaps selfishly, decided that her worries must be unfounded, after all.

5

La Starina was in fine voice that night, or so everyone assured each other. Had she ever hit those top notes so divinely before? Had the vibrato in her last, echoing moments ever been so affecting? Surely not!

Polly, having retreated to the small chair in the farthest corner of the box during the interval, fanned herself, and wished the evening might end. She was hot and unsettled, and she felt a head-ache coming on.

It was one thing, she thought, to dance lightheartedly at a ball or Assembly, knowing that despite its many attractions, the true purpose was to present a young lady to prospective partners, not unlike a bullock at a country auction. One could still take pleasure in the activities, and not worry overmuch about the outcome.

To sit in semi-darkness, framed by heavy brocade hangings, constantly being warned in anguished whispers not to fidget, knowing that so many eyes might be cast one's way, was maddening. It was especially so if one had to suffer through a tortuously convoluted performance of some ancient Imbrian legend performed completely in song.

The fact that La Starina was as lovely to look upon as her voice was to hear, was, moreover, spoiled by the fact that her romantic interest was sung by a portly man easily old enough to be her grandfather, and whose casting was apparently due to some other reason than talent. He hit several notes so piercingly flat that several people within Polly's view visibly winced.

From another perspective, the evening had begun well enough, although she was aware that her aunt would not have agreed.

Neither Mrs. Anwing nor Lord Valremer had been in evidence when they arrived. Eglantine did not seem aware of this, as she flirted mildly with Lieutenant Calthorpe after the ballet, and discussed the unseasonable heat with the Marquess of Gallerym as if it had never before struck her how odd the high temperatures were for this time of year.

Lady Mayland, on the other hand, was quizzing every seat in the Opera House, and becoming fretful that the one person for whom the new gown and the opulently decorated box had been organized expressly for, seemed to have decided to stay at home.

Eglantine had managed to sit beautifully still through the entire first act of the opera, looking as if nothing on earth could have pleased her more than this moment, although she also managed to murmur between unmoving lips that the lead tenor looked exactly like the old gaffer who brought the eggs up from the Home Farm at Mayland Manor. It was this observation that had brought on the reproof about fidgeting, since anyone within their orbit could have seen Polly's shoulders shaking with the effort of not giggling aloud.

The curtain finally came down on Act Two, and Polly, seeing the chance to no longer be required to imitate a marble statue, found her spirits rising. It was then that she saw the unmistakable silhouette of his lordship.

And even without looking, she knew that Eglantine had seen him, too.

It was not many minutes before a knock sounded at the door. And then it was only mere moments before she found herself moved away from her cousin's side by Mrs. Anwing, apparently desirous of retailing the latest rumour about a well-bred young lady who appeared to have made an elopement with one of her family's servants. It had taken no little skill to extricate herself from a conversation that held so little interest for her, and meanwhile, Valremer had asked for and obtained permission to walk with Miss Mayland in the corridor, where they might also procure some refreshment.

By then, the box was so overflowing with Lady Mayland's friends and Eglantine's entourage of hopeful young men, and the noise level had become so aggravating, that Polly had sought the shadows and found herself perilously close to weeping, although she could not have said why.

"Polly! What are you doing over there? Come and settle this question for me." Lieutenant Calthorpe was standing near the open door.

"Do you think," he continued as she came up to him, "Do you think that women ought to study archery? I say they are not meant for such pursuits, that it would be dashed unfeminine, but Bonica swears it is no such thing."

She gave a shaky laugh.

"Andrew, I would not like to quarrel with you…"

The lieutenant's sister snorted. "Miss Polly is too nice to you, Andrew. She will not tell you that archery teaches one any amount of poise and grace, and that you are positively Medieval!"

"Indeed," murmured Polly, vaguely. From her new vantage point, she could see the length of the corridor, packed with people milling about and snatching up glasses of lemonade. "I believe your sister has a good point. Archery does improve one's disposition, at least. Upon that you may rely."

She could not see Valremer or her cousin, but that was no wonder, given the crowd. She shifted a little closer to the door.

"Miss Calthorpe, I wonder if you might give me your arm? It is very close in here, and the lemonade looks very refreshing. Surely, you must want some, too?"

They stepped out into the throng.

"What a crush," said Bonica. "I declare, it is worse than ever. La Starina is all very well, but must the entire world attend on the same night?"

Polly made some sound of assent. She raked her eyes over the groups around the small tables and then down to the archway above the stairs. Not there. Not here, either, and there didn't seem to be anywhere else to look. The smallest tendril of apprehension curled about her heart.

"This way, I think," Bonica said, and still arm in arm, they moved towards a table where a black-clad woman was pouring out endless glasses of pale yellow liquid. Someone pressed one into Polly's hand.

And then, as she turned, she saw them. They were not far, just barely outside the shadow of a window embrasure, at the farther end from the stairs, and they looked as if they had been there for some time. Eglantine's face was turned up to Valremer's with a look of rapt enthrallment, hanging almost desperately on whatever words he was speaking.

On impulse, Polly moved forward, letting go of Bonica's arm, and saying heartily, "There you are, Eglantine! I swear I had nearly lost you in all this crowd."

Her cousin started, as suddenly as if Polly had shouted in her ear, and turned, almost with relief.

"Oh, Polly, what good timing! His lordship was just saying to me... was just telling me - that is, reciting some verses! Polly is the expert, you know, for her father was a most accomplished poet."

"Indeed, I do know it – how could I not? Lowell Mayland was quite justly famed in his day." But he said it mechanically, meeting Polly's gaze with a hard, appraising look that quite unsettled her.

"Never mind that," said Bonica, suddenly. "The bell's gone for the next act. You don't want to miss anything, do you?"

And Polly, who had always found Andrew's sister to be opinionated, brash, and somewhat annoying, fell rather in love with her just for a moment. Valremer let go of Eglantine's wrist, smiled most pleasantly, and escorted them amiably back to Lady Mayland's side.

ON THE ROAD leading out from Summerpoole, a man stood quietly in the shadow of the trees, waiting. It was late, and he would have much rather not been there at all, but this was another meeting he knew he must not fail. Presently, he heard the sound of horses' hooves, and, when a lone rider came into view, he stepped out onto the verge.

The rider reined in and dismounted.

"Well, this is a merry meeting," Jack said, grinning. "I take it you have news, then?"

"Aye," said Joe, hoarsely, and then cleared his throat. "Aye. I did like you said, Jack. He's still on the hunt, seemingly."

"Excellent. And did he sound suspicious, d'ye think?"

"Nay. He weren't at all sniffy at it. Said we'd have no call to worry over the Excisemen, either. Which," Joe added, "is what I would believe, any road. I'd not cross that one, Jack, not for all the gold in Gauderaude, and that's a fact."

"Hah! Well, and you need not. If there's crossing to be done, it's his lordship that will do it. I know his kind."

Joe sighed inwardly. Jack had that voice again: the voice of someone too mad to know fear. Jack didn't know what the lord was like. He hadn't seen those cold, pale eyes or heard the steel under the velvet in that voice.

He thought, not for the first time, that he ought not to have agreed to this. Not gotten himself or his boys mixed up in any of it. They should have stuck to what they knew, which was bringing in little bits of harmless occult contraband to sell to hedge-wizards, and the odd enchanted parasol that gentlewomen with limited means could only afford at smuggler's prices.

It was too late now. They were in it up to their necks, for good or ill.

But he made a promise to himself, in that dark night on the road, that if ever he got free of this with a whole skin, he'd never go within a hundred miles of the gentry again.

No, nor Mad Jack, neither.

6

T he Duchess had had to restrain herself for a full half-day before sending word that Lady Sackler was all kindness in thinking of her and that she would be delighted to attend a concert-party. She was no great admirer of the rather insipid music that Master Canina wrote, but so incredibly tedious had her lonely evenings at home become that she remarked to her son that she would have accepted an invitation to a Lecture on the Great Southern Ape's Eating Habits, if that had been on offer, for the sheer pleasure of seeing someone else's drawing-room curtains.

"Are you so blue-devilled, Mother?"

She shook her head.

"Not blue-devilled, Jarod. It is only that one cannot go out in society in precisely the way one was used to, you know. I expect when the Season ends, and we go down to Ambridge, I shall do very well, and next year, you know, we shall not be expected to wear our hearts on our sleeves."

"Well, I hope you do not want me to squire you to this fandango. I own I would rather be torn to pieces by those Southern Apes than to spend my night at such a dull affair. Is there not some other occupation that the world would not frown at, something that you might actually enjoy?"

"No, no, you need not trouble yourself about me. I expect Hermina will volunteer to come for me in her carriage. You know how she loves to manage people's affairs - I need only drop the tiniest hint!" She smiled. "And I do not go for the music, in any case. It will be pleasant, I think, to see some different faces, for you know, the Sacklers always know everyone worth knowing."

IT HAD, all in all, been a rather quiet, perhaps even dispiriting, week for Lady Mayland, since the opera.

They had not seen Lord Valremer at all: he did not call, and merely sent his regrets for the card-party Lady Mayland had arranged "to please the gentlemen", as she had put it. Nothing, she believed, was more enticing to the Male of the Species than to make wagers on Chance.

The party had gone off well, even so. The older guests had played whist with the quiet concentration that this always engendered. The younger folk had begun with cribbage, but when that inevitably palled, Lieutenant Calthorpe had suggested a round or two of Sorcerers' Straws. The concentration required them each to levitate the narrow strips in turns, and the attempts to thwart each other's little incantations found so much favour and hilarity that it was quite twelve o'clock before they could be persuaded to leave off and have some supper.

They had seen little of Valremer's cousin that week, as well, although that had troubled Lady Mayland much less. Mrs. Anwing had waved to them as their carriages passed in the Park, but did not pull over to chat. At the Westerland cotillion, she was certainly all smiles, but only stayed by their side long enough to allay their suspicions about the story that had been abroad, regarding a certain young lady's runaway match.

"My dears, nothing could be further from the truth. I had it from the Countess' own lips. The girl came down with a putrid throat, and the Earl only took his curricle in order to catch Doctor Chambard before he went into the country. I swear I do not know how people can be so ill-natured as to speculate on the worst, without the *slightest* cause."

They watched, then, all of them breathing unconscious sighs of relief, as they were left in a swirl of silk skirts and Eau d'Ilrae, as Mrs. Anwing was swept off on the arm of a visiting Ambassador from Fendrais.

ON THE EVENING of Lady Sackler's concert-party, the Misses Mayland dutifully presented themselves in the Mayland House dining room, attired in frocks of cream muslin, newly adorned with the lavender ribbons from Collette's. Indeed, they had spent the afternoon removing the more sprightly colours the gowns had originally been trimmed with and adding these respectful shades acknowledging bereavement.

Lady Mayland spent no little time inspecting her charges' appearances. She earnestly regretted that lavender hair ribbons most assuredly did not suit Polly, which meant that they had had to be changed out for a subdued ivory that did not instantly declare war on her rebellious curls. She then felt moved to discourse at length on the odds of the Dowager Duchess indeed feeling strong enough to support an evening of even this level of subdued gaiety, so that the Maylands sat down to a light repast much later than planned, and by the time they reached Sackler House, they were only barely in time, and just managed to find chairs and settle themselves before the concert began.

The music was, predictably, so unexceptional that its real use was to offer convenient conversational gambits when the concert portion of the evening was over and the guests were able to mingle and exchange the latest news.

Lady Mayland, as soon as she stood up, had her attention claimed by Lady Sackler, who wished her opinion of a new kind of Floating Aromanthia shrub she had recently obtained from the Continent. Meanwhile, Mr. Wisley's sister had linked arms with Eglantine and borne her off to the end of the room where a few of the younger guests had gathered, and Polly, having stopped to pick up and return a silk shawl to its elderly owner, found herself momentarily alone in the crowd.

She wandered over to the refreshments table. In this, her only aim was to appear occupied, rather than abandoned, and she was grateful, when an elegantly lady in a violet gown turned to her and smiled.

"You should try the nougat! I own, I am not usually partial to sweets, but this is something out of the common."

"I thank you," Polly said, smiling. "I admit, I cannot generally resist such things. My aunt worries incessantly that I shall come out in spots for it."

"My dear Miss Polly," said a familiar voice behind her. "I am delighted to see you! I made sure you would not arrive in time!"

The lady beside Polly looked up, over Polly's shoulder. Her expression was unreadable.

"And to see you here, Your Grace, and looking so well! It does my heart good to see it."

"Ah," said the lady. "Mrs. Anwing. I had no notion my health was of such concern to you."

Mrs. Anwing's laugh was brittle. "Oh, but you must know – of all things! But here, I quite forget my manners. Here is one who must be all eagerness to be introduced. Let me make known to you Miss Mayland – Miss Polyantha Mayland, that is."

"Indeed," said the Dowager, coolly. "But, as you might have surmised, Merelia, we have managed to scrape up our acquaintance without your help. We are united in our fondness for the Sackler nougat, as it happens."

Mrs. Anwing paled under her rouge. "I see you have recovered quite well," she muttered, but Polly, catching the Dowager's eye, knew the woman had not lowered her voice enough.

"La, and there is the Marquess, with my glass of punch," Mrs. Anwing added, rallying. "You will excuse me, I'm sure."

There was silence as they watched her flounce away.

"I beg your pardon, ma'am," Polly said, uncomfortably. "She is not usually so – so –"

"Maladroit, shall we say? Pray, do not think I hold you responsible for another's speech," said the Duchess. "But tell me, have you known Mrs. Anwing for long? I have heard, of course, that you are great friends with her."

"I would rather say that she is great friends with us," said Polly, then bit her lip. "I beg pardon, ma'am. I should not have said such a thing."

The Duchess patted her hand. "You need not fear to speak so to me, my dear. But I warn you: have a care with this. Merelia makes friends with no one but for a purpose, and that purpose is always for her own benefit."

"I know," said Polly, with some difficulty. "I am persuaded she is not safe. But what can one do?"

The Duchess regarded her with sympathy. "Just be careful, my dear. She means you no good, of that I am certain. Here, take some more of this nougat. I expect your friends will be delighted to share in it!"

Eglantine, having persuaded Mr. Wisley to move two chairs and a chintz-covered divan nearer to the window-seat, greeted Polly and the plate of nougat with enthusiasm.

It was a merry little party, and the odd note of urgency in the Dowager's voice, which had rather shaken her, receded. For a moment, it had seemed as though the Duchess was warning of something more than a public-set-down or a malicious rumour, but that, thought Polly, must be her own fancy. Nothing in what she knew of Mrs. Anwing suggested any more than that. Mrs. Anwing could be very tiresome, and occasionally rude, but that was surely no enormous sin. Many people were rude to others, even without meaning to be.

Really, when one thought about it, the Duchess had rather started it. Had she not been quite so cold, so close to snubbing Mrs. Anwing outright, the lady might not have been so rattled as to have retaliated, even in that whispered tone. It was not to be wondered at, not entirely.

And so, when Mrs. Anwing joined their little group, taking advantage of the confusion of sending the gentlemen off to procure glasses of punch, to sit down next to Eglantine on the divan, Polly was inclined to view her more charitably than she might otherwise have been.

For a moment or two, the conversations flagged.

Mr. Wisley, bearing a small tray of tiny punch-glasses, claimed her attention. She turned to take the offered refreshment, and from behind her, she heard Eglantine, always one to observe the niceties, remark on a pretty bracelet that Mrs. Anwing was wearing.

"The merest trifle," Mrs. Anwing said. "But it would match your hair ribbons exactly. Here, let us see it on you!"

Mr. Wisley, in much the same vein, resorted to his usual gambit and asked Polly what the hunting around Mayland Manor was like.

From behind her, Polly heard a stifled gasp of pain.

"Oh, dear!"

Eglantine was lying back against the cushions, her face quite pale. On her lap lay the silver and amethyst trinket, and she was holding out her arm. A long red scratch, bright with drops of blood, now adorned her wrist.

"Oh, my dear, how wretchedly stupid of me! I cannot think how I came to be so clumsy!" Mrs. Anwing was, if anything, more distraught than Eglantine. She whipped out a silk handkerchief from her reticule, and began dabbing at Eglantine's wound.

"How awful!" Miss Wisley said, with sympathy. "Dear Miss Mayland, have you need of my *charm volatile*? I vow, you are quite pale."

Eglantine sat up, with some force.

"No, no. Indeed, I am perfectly well, Miss Wisley. It was only the surprise of it! Pray, do not make such a fuss, Mrs. Anwing. It is the merest scratch. Look, it is not bleeding at all now."

"Oh, but you must be quite shattered," said Mrs. Anwing. "Here, I beg you, take my punch-glass. I haven't yet touched a drop. A sip or two will set you up, I am convinced."

Polly moved to Eglantine's side.

"Dearest," she said. "Are you quite sure you are all right?"

"Of course I am, you goose." Eglantine slipped her wrist from Mrs. Anwing's grasp. "You see? It is quite on the mend already."

"Well, then," said Miss Wisley, "There's an end to it. Do you go to the Traumerie ball next week, Miss Mayland? They say the Fireworks will something like, at least. The Countess has a Talent for them, or so I have heard."

7

P olly, having formed the intention of changing out some books at the Subscription Library, forced herself to wake early the next morning. Barely a soul was stirring, save for the housemaids, and the thought of a half-hour's worth of utter solitude was simply too enticing.

Having breakfasted in companionable silence with her uncle, she waited only until he had departed for his club before collecting her books and donning a very pretty chip hat with tiny lilies coaxed into bloom along the brim, and then slipping unnoticed out the front door.

The air felt beautifully cool, and, since she was able to cross through the park into Honeysett Street, it was blissfully quiet. Save for a few servants, a vagabond or two, and the occasional fishmonger crying their wares along the pavement, the streets were empty.

At the top of the walk, there was a tall man in a ragged woolen greatcoat, but she barely registered his presence. A watchman, she supposed, or some sort of tradesman.

Once at the Library, she was forced to stand in an annoyingly slow-moving line, behind an elderly governess accompanying two impatient, fidgeting little boys and holding a long list of requests for various titles, as well as a young man whose outmoded coat suggested he had seen better times, and whose taste ran to extraordinarily obscure tracts on History.

Moreover, the volume of Friesian's "Artifices", which Master Sempervirens had recommended to them as suitable for study, had still not arrived, and Polly had, perforce, to take the Librarian's suggestion of another, less-well known treatise, entitled "Arcane Alchemies and Their Artefacts", which she found to be small, shabby, and rather grubby around the edges.

By then, the day was proving to be every bit as hot as the days that had preceded it, and she dawdled under the trees in the park, where the sun had made little progress. It took some effort to move on from the quiet shade and step out into the sunny street.

The man in the greatcoat was standing on the corner, only two houses away from Number Four. There was something peculiar about that: what would a night-watchman or a tradesman be doing, lingering without purpose in Shalliton Place? She stepped back into the shade of the overhanging trees, and studied the man.

It was odd, and not only because wearing a woolen coat seemed to be the height of folly in this abominable heat.

He seemed familiar to her, which was ridiculous, and he seemed to be watching her, which was not ridiculous – it was impertinent.

Polly turned, precipitately, with the sudden resolve to ignore the man's existence, and in her haste, slipped on the curb. There was an instant, sharp pain, and she sank, suddenly and heavily, onto the pavement, with a little cry of anguish.

"Miss? Look here, miss – "

She felt a strong arm under her elbow, but her sight was blurred with tears, and as she blinked to clear them, the door to Number Four, Shalliton Place burst open and one of the footmen ran out shouting.

"Here, you, let her be!"

The footman was there, and the strong, comforting support at her side vanished. Moments later, when a second servant had joined them, and she was being solicitously shepherded across the road and up the steps, she began to look around for that kind savior, but saw no one in the street at all. Not even the man in the greatcoat.

It was, in the end, only the mildest of sprains. Within moments of gaining the entrance-hall, she began to recover herself, and was able to hobble quite competently to the breakfast-room. Minutes later, the pain was completely gone and she was apostrophizing herself as a pea-goose, and begging the servants not to mention the incident to her aunt.

Thus, when Lady Mayland at last gained the breakfast room, she found her niece seated there, seemingly completely at ease, her hat flung onto an empty chair, and her attention fixed rather doggedly on the latest issue of the *Gazette*.

"Why, whatever have you been up to, pet? It's not gone Morning Bells."

"Walking," said Polly, carefully truthful. At the Home Farm, she had been used to long, solitary walks, since it was obvious no real harm could come to her there, where everyone knew her. Wandering about the streets of the City alone, however, was strictly prohibited. Still, she was confident that Lady Mayland was unlikely to inquire too deeply into the matter. "I changed out our books, Aunt Mayland. The 'Dark Lady of Gwent' has come in, and I knew you wished to read it, so I brought it along."

"How sweet you are," her aunt said. "Although when I shall have any time to read, I do not know. The Season is so fatiguing for someone who is used to more quiet pleasures. Ah, well, you girls come first, that's what I have always said, and I mean it, too. I expect once you are married, I shall have plenty of time to enjoy many quiet evenings. "

Polly smothered a giggle. Lady Mayland's notion of a quiet evening ran to dress parties of upwards of fifty persons, and even when in residence at the manor, she rarely sat down to dine without at least a half-dozen guests. It was most likely that 'Dark Lady of Gwent' would, like so many books before it, languish unread on the side table in her drawing-room until it fell out of fashion, and a new title was the talk of the City.

"I should get Annie to look out your new walking dress for you, Polly," her aunt said, after a moment. "We are promised to Cousin Albertine for tea today. Tedious, I know, because she will want to tell one everything one is doing wrong, and finds fault with every new fashion, but I did promise your uncle that we would not neglect her, and I never go back on my word. At least, not without reason, although being forever criticized about one's clothes and jewels and what people one knows ought to be reason enough, I should think. I hope I can find something to wear that will not set her back up, but I fear that is not likely. I never knew anyone so disagreeable – oh, Polly, I pray you won't repeat that to your uncle! He would be so distressed!"

"Indeed, I will not, Aunt Mayland," said Polly, laughing. "I quite agree with you. Cousin Albertine always makes me feel as if my boots are unbuttoned, or that I have used the wrong spoon for the soup!"

"It isn't funny, Polly."

"What isn't funny?" asked Eglantine, as she came through the door.

"Nothing," said Lady Mayland.

"Cousin Albertine," said Polly, at the same moment.

"Oh," said Eglantine. "Oh, that's right. Mamma, *must* we go with you? Cousin Albertine's house is so stuffy at the best of times. It is sure to be quite stifling in this heat. Can we not cry off?"

"I wish we might," said her mother, regretfully. "But it is quite impossible. I have put her off twice already. Well, there was the exhibition at Merrill Gardens - we could not have missed that. It would have been most shocking to have done so. And then we'd already promised Mrs. Wisley to accompany them to the musicale last month, so how we could be in two places at once, I do not know. In any case, I gave your father my word we would go today, and so we must, my loves."

"Doomed," said Polly. "We must take the rough with smooth, Eglantine. You, at least, she admires for your looks and quiet manners. I expect she will ask me again why my hair is so very *colourful*, as if I were growing it this shade just to upset her."

"Perhaps," said Lady Mayland, hopefully, "perhaps it will not be so very bad. She is getting very infirm, and tires easily, or so your father says, Eglantine. One can hope, if we are very careful, she will not find quite everything about us so disturbing."

Alas, either Lord Mayland was mistaken in his estimate of his cousin's health, or else she had rallied considerably since his last visit. No sooner had the ladies had sat down in the very upright and outdated chairs in her drawing-room, than Miss Albertine Mayland remarked that Polly's complexion was very sallow-looking, and that she was shocked that Lady Mayland allowed it.

They nodded obediently and murmured assent, as that was the only response that ever seemed possible in these exchanges, and they nibbled the slightly stale bread spread thinly with butter, accompanied by the weak tea Cousin Albertine claimed to prefer.

"That Ryssington boy – I hear you have hopes of him, Polyantha." Polly began to protest, but Cousin Albertine ignored her. "Zephanine, you would be wise not to entertain any notions in that quarter. Ten to one, there will be another War, and he will very likely die. He's a hothead, like his father, and Polly would be left a penniless widow. I don't say it ain't likely, whoever she marries, but you should at least make a push for something better."

"I assure you, Cousin –" but Albertine was already moving on. "What are you wearing, Eglantine? That hat is most unbecoming. Young girls should never wear velvet. In my day, you would have been refused the doors at the Assembly, if you were seen about in anything so vulgar."

Since those days had to be all of fifty years gone by, it was on the tip of Polly's tongue to point out that quite possibly, Cousin Albertine needed to step abroad more often, and see what people actually wore nowadays, but Lady Mayland caught her eye, giving her a wild look, and she subsided into decorous silence.

At length, having had every item of clothing criticized, and all of their closest acquaintance abused, they took their leave, and climbed back, subdued and depressed, into the landaulet.

"Well, at least we need not go again until the end of the Season," said Lady Mayland, when they had at last rounded the corner out of sight.

"I," said Eglantine, "do not intend to ever step one foot inside that mausoleum again. Mamma, it is the outside of enough. She called Belinda Wisley a *mushroom*!"

"I know, my love. I know. Indeed, it is very trying. But your dear Papa feels so very sorry for her. She was much in love with a young man who was at the Academy, but her father wished for her to make a grand marriage and forbade them to ever see each other again. And no other men came up to scratch, you know, so she has not had a happy life."

"Oh," said Eglantine, and blushed. "Indeed, that is very sad, and very cruel, too. I hope no one would ever do so to me!"

"Would that I could be the breeze, that loves the fairest flower of spring..."

The letter had the look of age – it had been read and reread, folded and refolded, and several times thrust into pockets or stuffed into escritoire drawers, so that now, no matter how one tried to smooth it out, there were places where it was quite faded and unintelligible.

It hardly mattered. He could have recited every word perfectly.

What he could not have done was to make sense of its contents. Lowell Mayland's words had been quoted along with other poetry and similar trifles in an uncharacteristically hasty scrawl, and perhaps from a disordered mind...or else the message had been obscured for other reasons. Neither the first nor the twenty-first reading had shed much light regarding its meaning.

Until now.

8

Major Everard was no stranger to the alleyway that ran behind the barracks of the Home Guards. It was a popular place for younger officers, both for the quiet of it, so unlike the rowdier mess-hall inside, and for the privacy afforded when trysting with a ladylove who might not be quite suitable for more refined surroundings.

He was not at all surprised when he was not met by an open greeting, but was compelled to wait for some minutes, idly smoking his cheroot, until a figure detached itself from the shadows and made its way towards him.

"Your Grace," he offered, and then, abandoning these formalities, said, "Powers, Jarod, you look exhausted! Did you ride from Summer-poole today?"

""Why not? There was little to stay for. It's as we thought, you know," added the duke. "Austin was not lying. Valremer still thinks the glyph is in transit, and he means to have it yet."

"It might help if we knew, ourselves, where the confounded thing has got to. Are you sure your brother did not leave even the barest hint?"

"Well, as to that," said Jarod, "I believe I begin to see what he may have done. It's the devil of a coil, but I have some hopes, if we can string the blackguard along for a few weeks more."

"Can your man keep stalling for much longer, though? I own, I cannot like this. If Valremer should suspect...or if Austin should let slip your name – Jarod, this is madness. Best to trap Austin and warn off your little gang, and have done with it. That's all we meant to do, after all: get Austin dead to rights, stop Valremer from getting his bloody hands on the thing, and put their highborn smuggling days to rest. I'd say that was enough."

There was a silence.

"Not for me," Jarod said finally. "Not for me. Not anymore. I'll make the devil pay for what he's done."

"I TELL YOU, Mr. Jenkins, I don't know what to do, and that's a fact," said Mrs. Spry.

She was a small woman, Mrs. Spry was. Despite this, she was considered by the staff at Valremer Court to be a veritable Ogress and martinet, ruling over the footmen and parlourmaids, and even Cook, with an iron fist. Mrs. Spry bowed to no one below-stairs except the butler, Mr. Jenkins, although this was more a matter of form than substance. Jenkins himself was careful not to cross the housekeeper, especially when she was in one of her "moods".

"You'd best get Dolly up from the village," said Mr. Jenkins. "But it is a pickle, and no mistake. What does he want – opening up the house at this time of year? His father, Powers bless him, never did so. And us with no under-gardener till next spring. I've sent a message down to young Peterkin and if he won't oblige, I don't know what state the grounds will be in when his lordship shows up."

"Dolly? Much good that'll do me. Herself will find fault no matter what, but having Dolly underfoot will set her in a rage. You know what she's like, when things aren't just as she wants them. She do love to play at being the grand lady, don't she? I'll have to see if little Nan can do for us – at least she's a quiet one and don't cause no trouble.

But I tell you, Mr. Jenkins," the housekeeper finished up, "for two pins I'd hand in my notice tomorrow. Such ructions! I can't be having them – not now, with all the rooms to be aired and the linens needing mending before winter."

~

THE SEASON WAS PROGRESSING, despite the odd weather, as it always had.

In addition to paying a number of overdue calls, the Misses Mayland had been given a rather demure treat in the form of a picnic hosted by the Marquis of Gallerym, which took them out onto the Heath. The cooler breezes and shady trees did, in fact, do much to restore their spirits, which had been laid low by Lord Mayland's attempt to give their minds a more serious turn.

He had, possibly on the advice of Master Sempervirens, taken them to a Discussion on Ancient Amulets in hopes of improving their appreciation of the Arts Arcane. The motive was noble, and the lecturer both dry and longwinded - not to mention, rather alarming in his gloomy descriptions of the dangers inherent in dabbling untutored in these treacherous waters. They came home in still-subdued moods, but the Marquis' lavish hospitality soon put those somber feelings to flight.

The Grand Levee, tickets to which were rather limited, was the next, much-anticipated event, and one for which only Eglantine's position as the Season's acknowledged Beauty had gained them admittance: Lieutenant Calthorpe, by various maneuverings and no little bribery, had managed to secure three of the coveted vouchers for them.

It was a rather long afternoon, but the authorities had considered the continuing and uncharacteristic blazing sunshine, and erected awnings over the grandstands, as well as procuring additional ones to be placed adjacent to the tea-tent for the reception afterwards.

Lady Mayland, although she professed herself utterly fascinated with regards to military drills, dozed through the greater part of the display. Polly herself owned privately that after one or two exacting presentations, despite her appreciation of the skillful riding exhibited, she was close to boredom and drowsiness herself, but Eglantine, who had never before seemed at all interested in such endeavours, surprised them by showing the most intense and lively enthusiasm, mesmerized, apparently, by all two hours that the performances took up.

Lieutenant Calthorpe arrived, only moments after the last riders had galloped off to stable their horses, to escort them down to the refreshments' tables, a circumstance they had not expected, and Lady Mayland was further gratified when Andrew punctiliously presented them to all the commanding officers in the receiving line, before finding them a small table and seating in the crush of attendees. He then went off to procure them a nuncheon.

"What a nice young man," said Lady Mayland. "I knew his mother, of course – we came out the same year, I believe. Such a respectable family."

"He *is* kind, isn't he?" said Eglantine. "Miss Calthorpe is very sweet, as well. Only think, Mama, she gave up her ticket to us, so that none of us would be left out, and when I remonstrated, she only said that it would suit her best to make us happy!"

"Well, depend on it, my love, she will see levees many times over, if her brother stays in the Guards," Lady Mayland said, absently. "But indeed, we must be sure to thank her. Perhaps she would like to come to the Manor for a visit, after Midwinter? I am sure we could entertain her – it is usually so dull about that time, and having a guest would mean Lord Mayland could not possibly object to our giving a dance or two, do you not think?"

"Andrew, as well, could we not? That is, if he is able to take some leave? I am sure Papa would enjoy having someone to hunt with, if the weather is fine enough."

Lady Mayland, who had not, in fact, been paying very much attention to the conversation up till now, bent, as she was, on seeing which of her wide acquaintance had also secured tickets to this sought-after affair, turned to eye her daughter a mite more narrowly.

"My dearest," she said, then stopped. Lieutenant Calthorpe loomed back into view, bearing a large tray, with Captain Ryssington following behind, with a platter of cakes.

AND SO THE week passed in an unexceptional manner. Despite Lady Mayland's surprise and possible alarm at her daughter's attitude towards a hitherto innocuous and rather ordinary suitor, nothing more occurred to upset her belief that only a little more time would be required to bring Lord Valremer up to scratch. That Eglantine might not oblige her in accepting his addresses did not take serious root in her mind.

Their lives went on their customary way, for the most part without even the distraction of that distinguished admirer, as his lordship was rumored to have been called away to business in the country. No more was said of Lieutenant Calthorpe – Eglantine appeared to have forgotten her momentary interest in things military. Polly saw no more woolen-coated interlopers hovering in the streets, and, mercifully, no memories or ghostly voices disturbed her dreams.

Indeed, the only even mildly extraordinary occurrence all week was at the slightly wild evening spent at the Public Gardens, where they had been severely chaperoned by Mrs. Wisley, and had been taken away rather early, before the entertainments became too free for any delicately-reared gentlewoman, and even this, Polly thought, was really nothing much at all.

She had been dancing. They had, all of them, been warned to be very careful, since the company was so mixed, and not to allow themselves to dance anywhere except in the area directly in front of the supper-box the Wisleys had bespoken, but the figures of the dance were so energetic and the crowds so thick that she had, at the end of a March, completely lost sight of both the box and Mr. Wisley, who had led her out.

She looked about her in confusion, searching for some kind of landmark that might tell her which side of the open square she was facing, but the coloured lanterns drifting about cast unfamiliar shadows, and the vastly pretty topiaries all seemed much like one another now. That large shape there, depicting a winged lion? Surely that had been directly across from their box?

A woman in a scarlet mask bumped up against her and snarled, "Watch where yer goin', carn't you?" and pushed her aside. Turning, Polly lost sight of the topiary lion and began to search for it again.

A few yards away, there was a fat man in a grey domino, ogling her in a most unsettling fashion. She put on her sternest look, and then, to her horror, instead of being abashed, he began moving purposefully towards her.

She turned on her heel and began walking as sturdily as she could in the opposite direction.

"Excuse me, Miss?"

The voice was deep and resonant. She looked up.

He was rather tall, and draped in a black domino that showed off his broad shoulders. Between his mask and the shadows flickering in the crazy light, she could see very little else about him, but his mouth was set in a grim line.

"Miss, this is no place for you," he said. He took her wrist, very gently, and drew her forward. "Let me escort you back to your friends."

She felt no fear. Quite the reverse: she felt instantly reassured and utterly at ease as he began to lead her away from the shrubbery lining the edge of the square.

The world seemed curiously soft and unfocused, as if she were dreaming. It was like a memory – she was sure she had seen that mouth and heard that voice a thousand times before, and yet – he was no one of her acquaintance, of that she was certain. He might, she realized later, have led her anywhere.

The crowd parted and she saw her friends, right where they ought to have been.

The tall man let go of her wrist. When she turned to thank him, he was gone.

The fat man, on the other hand, was not.

She almost ran to the Wisley's supper-box, and was grateful when Mrs. Wisley announced shortly after that it was high time they were going.

Nothing – it was nothing. She had been introduced these last months to veritable scores of gentlemen, and he was, undoubtedly, someone at an Assembly or ball, or even one of her uncle's rather stuffy dinner parties. She had met so many people – she could not be expected to remember them all, and he did have a rather distinctive voice, which would explain both her feeling of memory and her trust.

It was only sense, after all.

LORD VALREMER DID NOT APPEAR in the City until the evening of the Wisleys' Cotillion, but it did not seem to Polly that her cousin was repining. Indeed, she seemed, if anything, in better spirits that she had ever been, and for that, Polly surmised, a certain Lieutenant could be held responsible.

Lady Mayland might note with relief that her daughter danced only once with Andrew at the weekly Assembly, and the world and her Mamma might see Miss Mayland as destined for a Great Match, but it was plain to Polly that Eglantine was beginning to have other ideas.

It was no surprise, when one thought about it. However much they might be enjoying the Season, both girls had both spent most of their lives in the country. It was not so unexpected that a quieter life, with all the pleasures of rural pursuits that she had grown up with, was far more suited to Eglantine's nature than some exalted and fashionable life could ever be.

While Lady Mayland had gone into the Supper Room with Lady Sackler, for refreshment and a little less of a Squeeze, Eglantine had, in fact, made her apologies to Lord Huntingfield, and sat out both the Reel and the Country Dance, spending those half-hours sitting with the Lieutenant on a settee, deep in what appeared to be a very serious conversation.

But at the Wisleys' ball, not merely Andrew, but all of Eglantine's court were as nothing once Lord Valremer arrived. He had swept through the crush around her as he always did, and with an adroitness no younger man could have possessed, convinced her to give up the March to him.

It was very odd, all the same. For one thing, Eglantine was not usually given to what amounted to rudeness by ignoring her dancecard, and for another, no matter how she tried, Polly could not keep her cousin in view. The March demanded she switch partners at the end of a measure, and she took the arm of a man in a patterned silk waistcoat, as he led her down the row of dancers.

"The heat is extreme, is it not?" he asked.

"Oh, yes," agreed Polly, absently. "Most enervating."

"And unusual."

"Indeed." She tilted her head sideways, looking vainly for Valremer's tall figure.

There was a silence.

"You know," said the man, sounding amused, "It's considered quite the thing nowadays, to speak to people during a dance. To be polite, you know."

"Oh!" She blushed. "I am sorry! It is just that – that..."

He squeezed her fingers, gently.

They had reached the end of the row.

"Over by the windows," he murmured. "You might want to look to your cousin. She seems uncommonly pale."

He handed her back into Captain Ryssington's care.

The music ended, and Polly, without a thought for propriety or even common courtesy, fairly ran to the end of the ballroom.

Eglantine did look pale. She was swaying, just a little, and all that might have been keeping her on her feet was his lordship, who had taken Eglantine's hands in his own, and was speaking to her in a low voice, even a whisper, in fact.

"My word, Eglantine! Are you unwell?" Even to her own ears, Polly knew she sounded almost panicky. "I am quite exhausted myself. Come and sit with me. "

LORD MAYLAND, still pursuing his notions of giving his daughter and niece a more serious turn of thought beyond the fripperies of their first Season, proposed, the next morning, that they visit the Portrait Gallery. Here, he assured them, they would not want for pleasure, since the building housed some very fine pictures of the Great Ones of the past, including some of their very own ancestors.

He was not entirely wrong in this. The paintings, dating as they did from many centuries gone by, showed very clearly the enormous changes in Fashion that had taken place. This, did he but know it, engendered huge amusement for the young ladies, although they managed to restrain their mirth and gaze with apparent solemnity at the starched ruffles and heavy, brocaded skirts of an early Lord Mayland, noting that the famous Wisley chin (a feature Belinda Wisley had undoubtedly inherited) was evident in their very earliest incarnations, and exclaiming with admiration on the handsomeness of the current Marquess of Gallerym when he had been but twenty years old and in command of the Brigade of Cannoniers who had led the victorious charge at Samaris at the very start of The War.

At the end of the Long Gallery, where paintings belonging to the most prominent families had been collected, Lord Mayland solemnly began to discuss, in markedly serious tones, the significance of the persons depicted there.

The House of Ambridge was, not surprisingly, he pointed out, well-represented. From the archaic and rather crude bit of fresco retrieved from an ancient ruin, showing the reputed ancestor of that House, to the more formal portraits of later times, the walls were a testament to the family's unique ability to remain at the forefront of History. Generals, statesmen, and no small number of Practitioners of the Higher Arts dominated the collection, of course, but in addition, several of their ladies had been prominent enough to have been officially recorded and hung with equal respect.

Polly listened with a sudden interest that she assured herself was due entirely to her brief conversation with Her Grace, and the kindness that lady had shown her. It was not, she told herself, in any way connected to her son or his romantic gift.

But when she came to the recently acquired likeness of that late noble, her heart sank.

He had been posed in the common way of these things, in a somber setting of a library, one hand resting on a carved wooden table covered with books, and he was looking not quite forward, but a little to the side and down, as if he feared his eyes might reveal too much.

There was, she thought, nothing in this that should have overset her. It was a perfectly ordinary picture, almost identical to a dozen she had seen this very day. It did not even look, when one considered it, very much like the man who had gifted her with a single rose at the Paltravers' ball.

Except there was something about it that tugged at her memory.

Something about the way he was standing, or perhaps merely the broadness and well-proportioned set of his shoulders – it was unnaturally familiar to her. Someone had seemed to her very much the same, in type if not in actual likeness, and very recently, too.

And that, she knew, was an impossibility.

IN THE DARKNESS of the Traumerie House gardens, an arc of twinkling golden stars swirled above the upturned faces of the guests, and then began to dance their way about in a stately pattern, forming a glowing sun. This Artifice then exploded into a flash of brilliance and proceeded to rain down tiny, manifest chips of gilt, cunningly fashioned into the shape of little Suns-in-Splendour, each one depositing itself onto the lap of an appointed guest, to the delighted exclamations of everyone assembled.

The Countess had outdone herself. The magnificent Fireworks and the little gilded trinkets were the least of it: there had been a Speaking Sculpture at the front door, which had intoned verses for each guest as they entered. There had been a Mechanical Orchestra to entertain them in the supper-room, and the ballroom had been illuminated by no less than ten witch-light chandeliers, imported at enormous expense from Gauderaude, and casting a rosy, happy glow on the proceedings.

Moreover, it was as if the Right Honourable Lady Traumerie had managed to cast an equal Enchantment on her friends, for everyone seemed to be wittier, handsomer, and more pleasant-mannered than they had ever been.

The Traumerie Ball always marked the height of the Season, and was not to be missed by anyone who could lay claim to an invitation. Even Cousin Albertine had emerged from her gloomy house in Romilly Park for the evening, attired in masses of stiff, brown taffeta and velvet in a style reminiscent of the previous century. She had even unbent so far as to admit that Polly was in decent enough looks, and that Lady Mayland at least knew how to spend her husband's money to advantage.

She then retired to a chair at the upper end of the ballroom, and sat beside an equally oddly-dressed foreign Prince who spoke no Imbrian at all, to survey, majestically, the proceedings below.

Meanwhile, her relatives plunged into this most glowing social occasion with real enjoyment.

Lord Mayland quite shocked his wife by standing up with her in the Quadrille as well as a Minuet, before abandoning the ladies for the card room. Lady Mayland regained her place on a blonde satin sofa, and fanned herself, quite pink with pleasure.

"I cannot think what has come over Mayland," she murmured to Mrs. Wisley. "I don't believe we've danced a Quadrille since, since - well, I don't know when!"

Meanwhile, Polly and Eglantine had filled their cards completely, and had given themselves up to what Polly referred to as utter dissipation.

When she had danced her fill in the Traumerie ballroom, and the fireworks had ended with every guest exclaiming over the souvenirs now clutched in their hands, it seemed to Polly that whatever had worried her in the past, it was done and dusted. Surely nothing in her

world could be amiss, when evenings such as these still came
her way.

She was just turning to remark on this happiness to Belinda
Wisley when a muffled shriek alerted her. She looked to the end of
the row of chairs and saw, to her horror, the knot of people bending
over a figure dressed in Maiden's Blush Oriental Silk, who lay,
unmoving, in the grass.

Polly pushed past her companions in an excess of terror. By the
time she reached the lawn, she saw that her worst fears were true.

Eglatine lay, waxen and pale on the verge, her breath coming in
uneven gasps. Doctor Chambard was kneeling beside her, feeling at
her wrist, and Lady Mayland had sunk down on the nearest chair,
trembling, her handkerchief pressed to her lips, and her face as white
as her daughter's.

The crowd was a blur. Polly slipped to her knees beside the
doctor.

"Please, oh, please, what has happened?"

"A faint," said someone. "But deuced odd, because it was just like
when Ambri–"

"Shut up," said someone else, sharply.

Doctor Chambard was chafing Eglantine's wrist, briskly. Her eyes
fluttered a little, and it seemed to Polly that her breathing was more
natural again.

"Please," whispered Polly. She looked at Doctor Chambard in
desperation.

Eglantine gave a faint little moan.

"Eglantine, dearest!"

"Nerves," said the doctor. "Seen it time and again. You young
people: burning the candle at both ends, out till all hours, and up
again to do all over. Lady Mayland," he continued, rising, "do not
distress yourself. She is merely fagged to death, and will come about
presently. But you must take her home at once. She needs rest,
and quiet."

A murmur of relief filtered through the crowd. Polly heard
someone call out for the footmen, and someone else suggesting the

Mayland's coach be brought around to the back, to save the poor girl a long trip through the house.

She could not take her eyes from Eglantine's face. She rather thought that she dared not do so. And yet, as if compelled by force, she found herself raising her eyes and looking out over the shocked and worried faces around her.

And there, beyond the gallery of friends and strangers, past the overturned chairs and trampled flowerbeds, she saw Mrs. Anwing, her mouth curving in a pretty "O" of concern, watching as if transfixed, staring at Eglantine's white, white face, as if she were unable to look away.

AT HER FINGERS, there trembled the singed and ashy remains of a lace-edged handkerchief.

9

Before the beginning of the present Season, Third Lieutenant Andrew Calthorpe had never had the slightest concern for his future.

He was not, he knew, the sort of man meant for greatness.

He did know himself to be of a suitable family, a long and honourable pedigree, and reasonable, if not exalted prospects. He took care to look smart in his regimentals, and to fulfill his duties to the letter, and he was, furthermore, of an easy disposition and got along with his fellow-officers very well. Beyond that, well, the Army was a comfortable place to be, and since the entire world was aware that he was his uncle's heir and possessed of a decent allowance from that gentleman, he had never found it difficult to raise the funds necessary to keep up with his wealthier friends.

It had been, until this year, a most pleasant and untrammelled existence, and one he had been supremely content with. He would, when the time came, cash out his commission, and settle into life as a country squire on his uncle's estate, and conduct himself exactly as his family might wish, tolerably amused by his horses and hounds, and , in some misty future, a suitable wife and the requisite heirs.

But from the moment he laid eyes on Eglantine Mayland, he had known that his simple ambitions would not serve, and that his entire future happiness depended on rising above the crowd that surrounded her. He knew that he needed something to put up against the wealth of Mr. Wisley, the startling good looks of Lord Huntingfield, or, even worse: the ancient title and undeniable charm of Lord Valremer.

He required, for the first time in his young life, something more than his pleasant disposition and the offices of his tailor. He needed some spectacular feat of heroics, or at least an indication that his military career was on the rise.

He had spent a considerable portion of his time hoping that there might be another War, where he might distinguish himself and be mentioned in Dispatches, or at least be able to entertain select auditors with the firsthand details of the battles reported on in the Gazette.

He had wracked his brains for ways to come into the notice of more powerful officers, in the hope that he might be given some little portion of even administrative limelight, since he had noticed before that this road, too, often led to promotion.

None of this was any good, of course: the treaty with Fendrais, now a full two years old, showed no real signs of being abrogated despite the rumours, and he confessed to himself that he had no head for the inscrutable details that administration required.

He had had to fall back on wishes and daydreams, and he was at least realistic enough to know that these were unlikely to bear fruit.

So he was more than a little surprised – apprehensive, even - when Major Everard, with whom he had only the most formal relationship, approached him on the morning after the Traumerie Ball and indicated that he would like a word in private.

"Got a job for you, Andrew," said the major. "A bit hush-hush, but I'm going to trust your discretion."

Lieutenant Calthorpe's heart leapt. Here it was. Like that story about Fate opening golden doors, the one his old tutor used to maunder on about: his opportunity was hammering at the gates.

But when the major began to explain to him what it was he wanted of him, his brow wrinkled in puzzlement.

"Watch over the South Coast Excise-men? Surely you don't think-"

"Never mind what I don't think," Major Everard said. ""I've got your orders here, and a brief for you. You're seconded to Summerpoole, as an aide-de-camp to Captain Austin. You just keep your eyes and ears open, young man, and if you come across anything – anything at all, mind! – that strikes you as odd or worrying, you send word to me. I've written it all out for you."

"Yes, I see," said Andrew, not seeing at all. "Yes, of course."

"You read up my notes and memorize them, and then burn them. And don't speak a word to anyone. The story is that you've been assigned to this because you know the area. Your family has a place near there, don't they?"

"Well, my uncle does, yes. Spent quite a few half-terms and summers there, as a matter of fact. But the thing is, sir –"

"Nothing to it. Ten to one, it'll be a bit of a holiday for you, and you'll get a nice addition to your service record, to boot. You do want to get on in the Regiment, don't you?"

"Of course I do," Andrew said, fervently. "You can rely on me sir. I won't let you down."

"I'm sure of it. You come of good stock, Calthorpe. But mind: no heroics. You're there to observe. Get to know the captain, and the others, too, of course. You'll write reports as often as you can, addressed to your Aunt Blanche, Blanche Moreau – it's all in my notes. You do right by this, Calthorpe, and I promise you, your way up the ladder will be a lot easier for it. I'll make sure of it."

And although the Lieutenant spent a number of anxious moments the next day, worrying over Miss Mayland's health (even to the point of arranging with his friend, Ryssington, to send flowers to Number Four on a daily basis, as well as messages about the Fair One's medical state to Andrew himself, at the Golden Sun, Summerpoole) he left the City with a heart considerably lighter than it had been for many weeks.

THE HOUSE in Shalliton Place looked gloomy and somber, even from the outside. Around back, there was almost constant turmoil, as the deliveries of flowers seemed unending, but the front showed only darkness behind the brocaded curtains.

Dr. Chambard descended from his carriage and turned to his driver.

"Come back for me in –" here he consulted his chrono-imp, "a quarter Turn."

The imp chirruped, and hopped onto the coachman's shoulder.

Neither Dr. Chambard nor his coachman were very fond of the imp. The coachman had been considerably happier in the days when his employer merely trusted him to return at approximately the requested time, without arcane assistance. The imp was rather insistent about making sure he was on exact time, even to the point where the driver had once had to leave a full third of a pint of cider undrunk.

Dr. Chambard disliked the imp because he frequently had the odd impression that the imp was watching him, but that was, of course, nonsense. It was a charmed entity, nothing more, and its only use was to keep time in order for him or his servants. Not that he had been unable to do so for many years without the imp, and he did, occasionally, consider giving it up.

On the other hand, it was an expensive little artifice, one that gave him an even greater air of successful competence, and since it had been a gift from a grateful patient, he felt oddly compelled to use it.

He turned and mounted the steps of Number Four with some misgivings.

He was still certain that Miss Mayland was merely suffering from an excess of nerves brought on by the exhaustion of her first Season. The symptoms seemed utterly ordinary and in keeping with this diagnosis, but he was troubled by her continued weakness and lassitude. It had been three days since she had fainted at the Traumerie Ball, and even allowing for the fact that she had suffered from a slight feverishness on the following day, he felt sure that she ought to have recovered herself by now.

∼

Upstairs, in the quiet of the sick-room, Polly's thoughts ran on much similar lines.

Eglantine, for all her fragile beauty, had always enjoyed good, even robust, health. That she could be laid low by a few late nights or an excess of energetic dancing and flirtation had seemed unlikely to her cousin, but she had, that first night, pinned her hopes on Dr. Chambard's words. What else could it possibly be but fatigue?

She had been encouraged when, on the following morning, Eglantine had seemed to rally a bit, sitting up to sip her morning tisane. But then, not an hour later, she had begun to shiver and to complain of a megrim, and by the time the doctor had arrived, she was in the throes of a fever that did not seem at all connected to her swoon of the previous night.

The doctor had prescribed a healing draught that brought the fever down, but Eglantine had then slipped into a restless sleep, apparently troubled by intermittent dreams that left her more spent and weary than ever.

Polly could not be persuaded to leave her cousin's side, despite her aunt's tearful pleas and her uncle's stern observation that having both his daughter and his niece ill would be too much. A compromise was reached, whereby a small cot was set up beside Eglantine's bed, and Polly, somewhat mendaciously, promised to rest.

In the small hours of the second night, when Eglantine's breathing seemed to her to have slowed into something more regular, and Polly fancied that a little colour had come back into Eglantine's cheeks, she did lie down, but found her thoughts were not able to still themselves, and that her worries seemed to be increasing.

She got up again, and spent a few moments looking down at Eglantine. There was no appreciable change, and she felt that she ought to relax, yet knew that somehow, she could not. She glanced around the room, which was filled to overflowing with those deliveries brought up from below-stairs: masses of flowers, out-of-season fruits in beribboned baskets, and books of uplifting verses to be read to the Non Pareil , if she should need distraction.

On the bedside table, along with a stack of gilt-edged missives from various admirers, two bottles of scent, and three handkerchiefs, lay the silly little book the Librarian had insisted Polly must take away instead of "Artifices".

The type had been set in a very old-fashioned style, cramped and with ornate flourishes, which made it rather difficult to read, but that was all to the good. Polly had to concentrate quite hard on the flowery passages describing some ancient Magicks, prose that seemed determined to shock its readers, but with so many decades' distance between the writer and Miss Mayland, served only to engender amusement.

"What a lot of ninnies our great-grandparents must have been," she thought. "And so petty and mean-spirited. I swear, they thought of nothing but impressing others and getting tiny revenges on their rivals. Indeed, I think they must have been quite mad. No wonder Cousin Albertine is so sour, if this is the way people went on when she was a girl."

She leafed through several pages. There were a great many more items that served to shore up her belief in her ancestors' silliness: Chaunts and Charms for "Gaining A Gentleman's Attentions", for example, as well as a Potion to induce a servant to do extra work for no increase in wages.

The last section of the book proved more than a little soporific. There was an addendum on the power of certain Rare Herbs, useful not only for the previously-mentioned malicious Charms and Enchantments, but also, in an attempt, perhaps, to garner some extra notoriety, a list of more powerful and malignant Plants. The rather convoluted text warned that their use was most strictly curtailed by Law, and that their descriptions, along with the very detailed illustrations, were meant only as cautionary information, and to give the reader the ability to stay well clear of all of them.

The accompanying anecdotes illustrated the dangers inherent, but they were curiously dull, owing to the old-fashioned language employed. Polly's eyes closed at last, and she was only awakened when the second housemaid brought in a tea-tray and opened the curtains to the bright light of the morning.

Eglantine was still sleeping. Was it her imagination, or was that sleep more peaceful than before? Polly listened carefully to the sound of those even breaths and hoped, fervently, that it was so.

She was only partly convinced when Eglantine did wake, and sat up without any assistance, accepting a cup of tea without the least hesitation. She was still very pale, though, and Polly could see that her hand trembled, just a little, as she lifted the cup. Three days of rest had not restored her; not entirely, and that seemed ominous.

Dr. Chambard, she could see, was concerned as well, underneath his confident manner. He, too, she thought, was worried that this might not be some simple "fatigue".

And his parting advice, as Lord and Lady Mayland accompanied him down the stairs, dismayed them all even more.

"She needs better air. Country air, at least. Depend on it, she will do much better when she has quit the City. You'll see the roses in her cheeks, once she is resting comfortably in cooler climes."

THE NEWS that the most popular Beauty of the year might need to leave the City mid-season, even if only for mere days, brought a renewed storm of deliveries and a steady stream of callers, eager to offer their condolences and concern. Perhaps a few mothers of less entrancing charmers were relieved that their girls might have an easier time attracting suitors, but for the most part, the Misses Mayland were well-liked, and most of those who came were sincere in their commiserations.

On the fourth morning, the house was set into complete disorganization by the need to pack for an indeterminate stay at Mayland Manor. This circumstance was made even more fraught by the arrival of Cousin Albertine, who announced it as her duty to stand by her relations in their time of need.

"I knew," she said, by way of comfort, "That it would come to this. All that racketing about, Zephanine, and no regard for common decency. You cannot say I did not warn you. If I have said it once –"

But here, Cousin Albertine was interrupted by the opening door, and Mrs. Anwing appeared.

Although most of their acquaintance had been understanding of Lord and Lady Mayland's need for privacy and were content to write a few charming lines on the backs of the cards they left with the butler, Mrs. Anwing had refused to be denied.

"My dears," she said, dramatically, as the footman closed the drawing room doors behind her, "My dears! I come to you as a Messenger!"

Polly, having been persuaded to leave the sickroom and come down to partake of tea and toast, looked up in dismay. Mrs. Anwing ignored her and advanced on Lord and Lady Mayland with hands outstretched.

"Indeed, I have been in the most awful fret these last three days. But now we may set all our minds at ease!"

"I beg your pardon," said Cousin Albertine, in frostily regal accents. Mrs. Anwing ignored her, as well.

"Valremer, you know - well, I must explain, of course. Last night he chanced to meet Dr. Chambard at the theatre, you see, and at once enquired as to Miss Mayland's situation. 'Oh,' said the doctor. 'It's good air she needs, and nothing more.' And at once my lord asked if not sea air must be the best of all, and of course, the doctor quite agreed. So it is all settled, and you may rest easy on every count!"

"You have the advantage of me, ma'am," said Lord Mayland, sounding bewildered. "We leave for the West Country on the morrow."

"No, no, indeed, you shall not." Mrs. Anwing was positively aglow. "For my lord Valremer turned at once to me and said that we should put Valremer Court at your disposal, for however long you should need it, and that I must come at once to tell you. The Court is near

Summerpoole, you see, and what could be more beneficial? The sea air, you know! Miss Mayland will soon be in the pink again, and we will be only too happy to play host to you!"

"Sea air? What has sea air to do with it?" Cousin Albertine's tone was, if anything, more glacial than ever. "She will do very well in her own home, where her *family* may look to her every need."

Mrs. Anwing seemed immune to the ice.

"Oh, but you must know – sea air is always considered the most healthy thing! Indeed, we inquired of Dr. Chambard most particularly."

Afterwards, Polly remembered only that whatever words she, Cousin Albertine, or her uncle might have said died on their lips, for at this point, Lady Mayland burst into tears.

"So good of you," she managed, between sobs. "So *very* good of you. Oh, and it would be the perfect thing, I know it!"

There was the scent of honeysuckle, and something spicier and even Cousin Albertine seemed to have lost the power of speech, for once. Polly herself found that she could not raise her eyes from the tea-table.

There was the voice of Lord Mayland, begging Mrs. Anwing to convey to his lordship their grateful thanks. There was some discussion of times and road conditions, and the sound of the drawing room doors opening, then closing once again.

There was, very briefly, some silence.

"There," said Lady Mayland, triumphantly. "Did I not say it? Depend on it: we shall be announcing her engagement before the month is out."

10

It had been agreed, of course, that the journey down into Summersett must be accomplished in easy stages, so as not to tax the waning energies of the invalid, but even so, there had been in Mrs. Anwing's instructions a definite note of urgency, a plea not to put off their journey for any longer than was necessary.

Still, the change in plans had caused some significant delay.

For one thing, it had been imperative to soothe Cousin Albertine's much-ruffled feathers, and, when an attempt to convince her that her affronted sensibilities might mean she would do best to stop at home signally failed, to agree to a rather later start to their journey, so as to accommodate her organizing her own household around her absence.

A great deal more of their late start was due to Lady Mayland's conviction, however, that there would be completely different requirements for a stay at Valremer Court than what had been deemed necessary for even a longish return to Mayland Manor.

For the Home Farm, only a few additional walking dresses and a pair of new boots for Polly had been added to her list of essentials. For a stay at one of the Nation's most admired stately homes, with such an ancient family name and history, there would need to be some not-inconsiderable improvements.

"I warrant you," said Lady Mayland, "Even a small family dinner will require some state. All the evening gowns, Fleurette. The jewels, too. And send someone to fetch the new slippers I ordered for Miss Polly, for she will need them if she wears her green satin."

Polly, spending most of her hours at her cousin's bedside, barely noticed the stream of instructions, pleas and last minute changes to the original plan.

After her initial chagrin, she had been persuaded by everyone that whatever else, the undeniable fact was that sea air *would* do Eglantine the most good: even Cousin Albertine was forced to admit this. Polly must put away her misgivings. Her aunt might see it as an opportunity to fix Lord Valremer's interest, but Polly's only concern remained Eglantine's speedy recovery. If spending a few days in the company of Mrs. Anwing and a man she distrusted only on the basis of old rumours and a vague sense of unease in his presence was the price of this, then she was prepared – even eager – to pay it.

In the end, it was not until dusk three days later that the two coaches turned into the long avenue leading to the Court. It was indeed a far grander place than even common report had made clear: silhouetted against an indigo sky streaked with scarlet, the high stone towers of the ancient castle stood out proudly, and each generation of Valremers had, in their turn, increased the grandeur and size of the original.

The visitors were only somewhat aware of the magnificence they were entering.

In fact, Polly scarcely remembered their arrival.

Over the last few hours, Eglantine's energy and spirits had flagged noticeably. Her family was conscious mainly of the relief they felt at the journey's end, and their gratitude for the way that they were received.

Mrs. Anwing, surprisingly low-voiced, gentle, and competent, shepherded them all into the great hall, up the stairs, and into their beautifully-appointed guest rooms so smoothly that they none of them had more than a moment to take in the grandeur surrounding them, and forever after, Polly could recall nothing beyond a small, dark-haired girl who unlaced her stays for her and helped her into an enticingly soft bed hung with dark green velvet curtains.

She was asleep almost before her head reached the mound of pillows.

~

DESPITE THE DEEP slumber and a late awakening, Polly still felt herself exhausted when she finally woke.

The little housemaid had brought her morning tea. She then opened the heavy drapes, and said brightly,

"Shall I unpack for you, miss?"

"Yes, of course." Polly watched as the girl opened the first trunk. Out came the new walking dresses, the half-boots and the hats.

"This for today, miss?" The girl held up one of the morning gowns for inspection.

Polly nodded. The maid laid out her toilette neatly on the divan beside the window and opened the next trunk, exclaiming over each evening dress as she unearthed them and hung them carefully in the wardrobe. She arranged the slippers, neatly matching them to each dress, and then brought out Polly's jewel case.

The bright sunlight seemed, for just an imperceptible moment, to dim. There was a bit of a breeze suddenly wafting through the tree-tops outside and Polly heard, she would have sworn, a familiar voice whispering through the leaves...

"Remember me..."

"Why, miss, whatever's the matter? Are you all right?"

~

SHE WAS LATE COMING into the breakfast room – Mrs. Anwing and Cousin Albertine were already there before her.

Her impression of the night before, that Mrs. Anwing was a rather different person here, where she felt, perhaps, more at home and confident, proved to be well-founded. Mrs. Anwing was all smiles and calm, and at pains to make her feel at ease.

"Do but make yourself comfortable, Miss Polyantha. And let me persuade you into some toast and an egg, perhaps? The kippers, I'm afraid, are a little cold, but I might ring for fresh ones, if you like."

Polly stammered, shaking her head. The egg would be fine. Mrs. Anwing did not press her further, but merely smiled lightly again, and said that she must be wondering at the absence of their host.

Cousin Albertine said, rather acidly, that it was no concern of hers. Mrs. Anwing only nodded, as if the elder Miss Mayland had said something wholly unobjectionable, and resumed her discourse.

Lord Valremer had asked her to make his apologies. Urgent business detained him until the morrow, but he had been at pains to leave word that they must consider the Court as their own. Every care for Eglantine's recovery would be seen to, and Lord Mayland, it seemed, had already gone out to try the fishing, which was rather well-spoken of by ardent anglers of the county.

"You must not think," Mrs. Anwing said, "that we have forgotten you, either, Miss Polly – I may call you that, may I not? Indeed, I have such plans!"

"It's most kind, I'm sure. But truly, Mrs. Anwing, you must not put yourself out for me. My only concern is for Eglantine's health. "

"As it is for all of us. But come, Miss Polly – she will soon be on the mend, and no young lady should be left to repine in solitude. There is so much in the neighbourhood to interest you, and no shortage of society. There is the Assembly, for a start, and I have made sure that all the local ladies will be only too pleased to make your acquaintance. I would not have it said that any guest here wanted for the slightest attention."

"I do thank you," Polly said. "Yet how can I think of amusing myself? I shall do very well, looking after my cousin."

"Nonsense, Polly," said Cousin Albertine, suddenly and alarmingly switching sides. "Your cousin has her Mamma, who, I agree, might be the most useless nurse in all the world, but is still her mother, and must be a comfort to her. Moreover, she has me. You need not trouble yourself. *I* shall make sure Eglantine has everything she requires, you may be sure of that. In your circumstances, you must take advantage of every opportunity, for who knows what eligible gentlemen might you meet here? No opportunity should be wasted, in your position."

Polly blushed bright red – a colour that had never suited her.

"You and I must get to know one another better," said Mrs. Anwing, stepping rather nobly into the breach of Polly's embarrassment. "Still, I fancy Miss Mayland is not entirely wrong. The City is all very well, but here, Miss Polly, you are sure to outshine any local girls. You will, I vow, be very much admired.

"There is one thing more I must speak of, however." Mrs. Anwing rose, and rang for the footman. "You are, of course, free to wander as you will – you must think of this as your home for as long as need be. But after sunset, we do caution you not to stray outdoors. At least, not past the terrace."

Polly looked at her in some confusion.

"The hounds," said Mrs. Anwing, vaguely. "They are let loose to roam after dark. For protection."

"But what can one possibly need protection from? Surely, the Court is not in any way at risk? And Summersett is reckoned a most prosperous and amiable place to dwell – or so I have always heard."

"Ye-es. Well, as to that, we have had an alarm or two recently. Thefts, you know. Attempts, at least, or so Valremer believes. But his lordship has trained up his hounds to guard us, and indeed, you must not have the slightest apprehensions. It is a precaution only, and certainly you will have no cause to leave your room at night. Merely ring for a servant: everyone here will be only too delighted to supply your tiniest need."

There was a rather awkward pause.

"Perhaps," said Polly, desperate to fill the gap, "Perhaps I will change, and go for a walk. I have heard the grounds here are accounted to be very fine."

"Indeed, and justly so. And now, forgive me, I must go and see to our domestic arrangements for the day."

"I knew it," Cousin Albertine hissed as the door shut behind their hostess. "I knew it – we shall all be murdered by footpads or robbed blind. The countryside. Apart from our own counties, I have always considered the countryside a mistake."

11

T he day passed pleasantly enough.

The reputation of Valremer Court's gardens was not in the least exaggerated – they were quite magnificent, in fact. There were long rows of willows to shade her path, wide expanses of artfully co-ordinated flower beds arranged simply to please the eye, and, as the fashion of a bygone era had once demanded, there was a folly made of dark-coloured stone, in the form of an ancient temple. It lay at the top of a hill, overlooking the ornamental lake, but Polly found she had no desire to go closer. It was, she decided, much too hot to climb up to it, and the building itself looked grim and inhospitable, and not at all what she would have called "picturesque".

It was some time before she found her way back to the Court, to repair to the sickroom, where she found her cousin to be in good spirits and with her colour returning. She still tired easily, and after little more than an hour, began to look drowsy, so Polly came away and sought the solace of Lord Valremer's well-stocked library.

At the sound of the first Evening Bells, she retired to her own chamber, where her aunt's very superior ladies' maid had laid out her evening dress and was waiting, with the little housemaid, Nan, to assist her.

That this was a vast comedown from attending to Lady Mayland was apparent in her every word and gesture. Fleurette made it plain that Polly was to regard this as a one-time experience, and proceeded to instruct Nan on how to arrange Polly's hair, which accoutrements went with which gown, and how the dresses must be kept and cared for, and then, at the earliest opportunity, decamped back to her mistress.

"You look lovely, miss."

Polly smiled. "You don't think it's a little too much for a quiet dinner?"

"Oh, no, miss. Mrs. Anwing always wears the most glorious things. Every night, miss, and never the same ones twice, even when there is no company at all. Which is mostly, miss. His lordship only has guests rarely here, especially since the summer. That poor duke, you know. He was here a good deal back then – not but what Mrs. Spry said that was all down to Mrs. Anwing having a partiality for the young man, as well she might – oh, miss, whatever's the matter?"

Polly had stopped, stock-still, staring blindly at her reflection in the mirror.

Ambridge here? This past summer?

"Remember me...for a little while..."

FOREVER AFTERWARDS, Polly could not, try as she might, bring to mind a truly clear picture of the days that followed their arrival at Valremer Court. They seemed to blur into each other, to melt into a haze of days that slipped away from her memory like beads slipping off a broken strand and scattering, haphazardly lost into the mist.

Lady Mayland had not been wrong in her predictions. Dining at Valremer Court was no casual family affair, and they sat down each night to fully nine courses consisting of clear soups followed by a dizzying array of fish, roasted game, at least three side dishes, and ending, always, with intricately decorated cakes and flavoured ices. These meals, too, blended their grandeur and variety into another blur of things repeated, over and over, one indistinguishable from another.

Some things stood out, of course.

Their host's return had been uneventful and pleasant, and Polly could remember wondering vaguely why she had felt so many misgivings about this invitation: Valremer was affable and charming to her all the way through the light nuncheon served up in the larger drawing room. She felt, in fact, rather guilty at having seemed to misjudge him: certainly there was nothing in his manner to suggest anything but kindness and solicitude for all of them.

But when she had changed her dress in anticipation of driving out with Mrs. Anwing, in order to pay a call to Lady Elias, who was considered one of the social arbiters in the county, she had gone down to the front steps to await her hostess, and there met his lord-ship, just coming up the drive.

She smiled tremulously, aware that she had not always behaved with perfect courtesy towards him, and faintly embarrassed by the recollection.

If Valremer remembered this, he gave no sign. He merely inquired after her plans, asked if she might convey his regards to Lady Elias, and hoped she would not find the local company too dull, after her time in the City.

She made some reply, still conscious of an internal but indefin-able constraint.

"Merelia has warned you about the dogs, I hope?" The subject seemed to come out of nowhere.

"I-Indeed, yes...," Polly stammered. "That is, she did say they run loose at night, for protection."

"Pray, do not distress yourself over it, Miss Mayland. It is merely that there are some questionable fellows about. The coast is always attractive to smuggling gangs, you see, and I do not trust them, when times are lean, not to turn to petty thievery instead. I am merely determined they shall not find the Court an easy target; that is all. My dogs are trained to sniff out strangers and make short work of them, of that you may be certain."

Perhaps it was only a cloud, that passed overhead. Perhaps it was only that the breeze from the rolling hills that lay out beyond those magnificent gardens picked up a little more strength. Perhaps it was only her imagination that added the tiniest note of menace underneath the pleasant words.

"As long as you do not stray outdoors after dark, you are perfectly safe...Ah! Here is my cousin at last." He turned, gave the pair of them a warm smile, wished them a pleasant day, and disappeared into the house.

Lieutenant Calthorpe, having presented himself to his new commander upon arrival in Summersett, found himself rather at a loose end in his position as aide-de-campe.

Captain Austin had seemed rather taken aback by his sudden appearance and his orders, but Andrew, in a moment of uncharacteristic inspiration, took the line that someone had it "in" for him at the Regiment, and that this had been a way for him to be gotten rid of. He managed, perhaps because his heart was not really engaged in the notion of subterfuge, to sound only the tiniest bit aggrieved, which had the effect of making it all feel, to Austin, to have a ring of truth a more pointed resentment would not have had, and he managed not only to find not a room at the already overcrowded Golden Sun for his new aide, but to consider quite seriously how best to utilize this addition to his staff.

The problem was that at the moment, there was so little to do. Austin made a point of drilling his men for at least an hour each day, and insisted on regular kit inspections, but since his sergeant did most of the real work, and since smugglers, it was well-known, were active primarily on moonless nights, and the choices for landing places in the district were so numerous, this, too, amounted to very little actual activity.

Austin himself declared he did not know the coastline well enough, and spent many of his waking hours out riding along the shore, looking for likely spots where a small boat might be able to come in without difficulty. Andrew might have assumed – in fact, did assume – that he would join in this enterprise, but Austin had shaken his head.

"You stay in town, Lieutenant. Someone needs to keep an eye on things here, after all, and the sergeant ain't the brightest of fellows, you know. And you can keep your ears open, too. The folk hereabouts know everything, and it might be they'll let slip a word or two. You hang about and make some friends: it won't be anything said outright, but who knows? You hear any oddments, you bring them to me."

Thus, Andrew found himself, as he later put it, spying in two directions. It was all very well, he thought, for the major to have listed out the kinds of things he might look out for, but since Andrew only spoke with Austin in the evenings when they dined together in the private parlour at the inn, and furthermore, had almost no contact with the squad of soldiers the captain commanded, it was hard to see how he could discover anything of use, always supposing there was anything at all to discover.

His attempts to woo the locals elicited nothing of interest for Austin, either. The innkeeper was taciturn and brusque, apparently in no way disposed to befriend him, and his son, Tompkin, was such a slow-top that it was rather like talking to a turnip.

Even the chambermaid, who had a rather red face and a permanent sniffle, was not inclined to gossip or flirt, and Andrew could scarcely make sense of the few conversations he had eavesdropped on in the common room. The local accent was positively barbarous, to his mind, and he began to despair of ever having anything to report on to anyone.

Moreover, he had received not a single word from Ryssington about Miss Mayland's health, and this worried him more than anything else could have. He began to imagine the most dire scenarios – that Eglantine was at death's door, and that his friend was trying to spare him the anguish...or worse: that she had recovered and that now any one of her suitors was fixing her interest, while the lieutenant kicked his heels in Summerpoole to no purpose whatsoever.

But well into his second seven-day, he was surprised by the sergeant as he was heading up the stairs to dress.

"Beggin' yer pardon, sir. The captain wished me to tell you it's full regimentals tonight. Gloves and all, he says."

Andrew managed to receive this information with aplomb, as if he knew what it might mean. He dressed with care, and made his way down to the parlour.

"Well, let's have a look at you," said Captain Austin, when he came through the door. "Yes, that'll do nicely. I expect you'll turn some heads."

"Sir?"

"It's Assembly night, Lieutenant. I go to every one."

Andrew nodded, blankly.

"It's work, you know. Don't go thinking you're in for a night of pleasure."

Andrew nodded, again, still mystified.

"The thing is," said Austin, confidingly, "the thing is that the gentry hereabouts is up to their necks in the trade. You mark my words – they know all about it, and half of them are in on it, one way or another. It's criminal, so it is – and you'll need to keep your wits about you. It's the young ones who are likely to let things slip – and they'll be more likely to talk when you're about than me. I've got hopes for you, my lad. Great hopes."

This speech had considerable effect on Andrew. He was sure, now, that Major Everard's suspicions of the captain were completely unfounded – nothing seemed to him at all insincere about Austin's desire to bring smuggling miscreants to book. He was conscious, too, of a desire to prove himself worthy of the captain's confidence in him. If they could break a smuggling ring – well, being in on that must surely do him credit.

～

Polly, at Eglantine's expressed wish, was doing a slow turn to show off her newest evening gown.

The need to balance her niece's unfortunate colouring with the strictures on proper, maidenly attire had quite overset Lady Mayland, when the Season had begun. In desperation, she had put Polly completely into Madame Honorine's capable hands, and that worthy had not failed her. The deep green satin underdress was elegantly Contrived to be most inconspicuous beneath the froth of sea-foam muslin, so that while, on initial glance, Polly seemed to be adhering to the rule that only pastel shades were acceptable for one's first forays into Society, the dress glowed from within with the intensity of an emerald, setting off her hair and complexion in a way that was quite riveting to the eye.

Cousin Albertine sniffed. "Those bangles are too grand for you, Polly. I fear you will set everyone's backs up, putting on such airs."

"Why should she not outshine everyone?" Eglantine asked, cheerfully. "She is a Mayland, after all. She must show us all to advantage."

Polly shook her head. "Indeed, I should rather stop here, with you, dearest."

"Goose! I am very much better – only just a little tired, still." Her hands plucked nervously at the sheets. "But promise me you will come in to tell me how everything is, when you come back. No matter how late, Polly – you can wake me. I won't mind."

"Nonsense," said Cousin Albertine. "She certainly will not do so. You may see her in the morning, when you are properly rested. I do not propose to have everyone traipsing in here at all hours, disturbing you. And so I told his lordship, when he said he would come up after supper. No gentleman would dream of visiting a lady in her bedchamber when I was a girl. I was minded to give him a set-down."

"Oh," Eglantine shrank back against the pillows. "Oh, did you do so, Cousin? It seems very odd – he is our host, after all."

"Well," said the old woman, grudgingly, "I held my tongue over that. But he will not trouble us again tonight, I fancy."

Polly, safely turned away from Cousin Albertine, rolled her eyes and saw Eglantine's lips twitch upward in amusement.

Yet underneath that, Polly was sure, her cousin looked curiously relieved.

~

DESPITE WEEKS of social engagements in the company of the most fashionable people in the City, and her natural desire to remain at Valremer Court ministering to Eglantine, Polly found that she was, at first, enjoying herself at Summerpoole's Assembly.

She had been besieged by introductions from almost the moment she crossed the threshold, and several younger ladies had been eager to quiz her regarding the latest fashions. Lady Elias' son declared himself quite smitten, much to Polly's amusement, since he did so before they had exchanged three words.

Still, whenever the conversation flagged or turned to local topics she had no interest in, her thoughts strayed back to Eglantine. They had been here a good few days. How many, exactly, she found herself unable to recall. Surely a seven-day, at least. Why her cousin seemed to still be so languid and tired was incomprehensible and worrisome, because Dr. Chambard had seemed so sure that only a day or two's rest would be needed.

And then it struck her as odd that she had not considered this before. She had, until this moment, not even seemed to notice how the days were slipping by with no improvement in Eglantine's health – but just as she began to think about what that might mean, an exclamation from Mrs. Anwing jolted her from her thoughts.

"Captain! How very good to see you again!"

Polly turned. The man Mrs. Anwing was greeting with such warmth was dressed in Excise Blues of extremely exquisite cut. He was not tall, but he held himself with authority and precision as he kissed Mrs. Anwing's hand and murmured that he was, of course, utterly charmed to meet with her again.

Mrs. Anwing began to introduce her, but Polly scarcely heard a word.

She cared nothing for an unknown Excise officer. It was the young man beside him that drew all her attention.

"Andrew!" she said.

He was staring back at her, open-mouthed.

The Captain said, "You must let me present my aide-de-campe, Mrs. Anwing. "

"Indeed, you need not – Lieutenant Calthorpe is well known to us, is he not, Miss Polly?"

"I am delighted to see you both again so soon," Andrew said, recovering himself a little. His voice was expressionless, and his eyes were still on Polly.

There was a slight commotion at the end of the hall, as the musicians sat down to begin the evening's selections.

"You'll give me the March, Miss Mayland, will you not?" Andrew's tone was suddenly urgent.

"Yes, of course – that is, if Mr. Elias will excuse my rudeness," she said, smiling across at her new admirer. "Old friends, you know, Mr. Elias. I will give you the Quadrille, in exchange!"

She put her hand on Andrew's arm.

"Andrew! How do you come to be here?"

"I might ask you the same, Polly! Where is Eglantine? How does she do?"

"She is – that is, I think – oh, Andrew, she is well enough, but still greatly fatigued."

"But how do you come to be here, Polly? I don't understand. I should have thought-,"

"We are guests at Valremer Court," she said, with some difficulty. Only as the words left her lips did the strangeness of this sink in to her.

The music began, and they followed the couple ahead of them as they stepped through the figures, hardly heeding their feet.

"It was thought the sea air would do her good," Polly said. She turned and curtseyed to the gentleman on her left.

Andrew bowed to the girl beside him.

"And whose idea," he said, turning back, "whose idea was that?"

They linked arms and proceeded up the hall.

"Valremer's," she said, faintly.

They came to the top of the line. Polly exchanged places with the young woman across from her, linked arms with the man she'd just bowed to, circled, and was handed back into Andrew's care.

"Tell me," he said. "Tell me, Polly: is there any hope for me at all?"

They began the long march back down the row of couples.

"She is fascinated by him," said Polly, softly. "She seems to find him interesting, I think – in a dangerous kind of way. But – oh, Andrew, I do not believe her *heart* is engaged!"

12

S he slept late the next day, which was odd, because they had come away from the Assembly quite early, owing to the distance from Summerpoole to the Court, and to Mrs. Anwing complaining of a slight head-ache.

Left to her own desires, Polly would have stayed to the very end. After that first dance, she exchanged no more than two words with Andrew, although she had tried to. Indeed, it felt almost as if events were being contrived to keep them apart, for Mrs. Anwing became even more gracious than before and introduced the lieutenant to positively scores of young ladies. Being a very well-brought up young man, he had naturally asked each of them to dance, and even during the Interval, those good manners and the instructions he had had from Captain Austin kept him from her side.

But by the time she had dressed and breakfasted the next morning, the whole evening seemed to have acquired a kind of faded feeling, as if it had happened some time ago, and although she described her evening's entertainment to her cousin a little later on, she very nearly forgot to mention Andrew's presence in the neighbourhood.

Eglantine's reaction startled her, even so.

"Lieutenant Calthorpe? Here?" Eglantine sat up, and her cheeks were pink with pleasure. "Do you think he might call upon us?"

"Well, as to that, dearest, I do not know." Polly paused. She rather thought that Andrew had said something about visiting, but she could recall nothing definite. "He has his duties, you know. It might not be possible..."

"But surely we could invite him to do so, at least? I am so much better already. Surely we should not be so discourteous – and his lordship did say we were to consider ourselves at home here! Promise me you will write to him immediately, Polly."

POLLY WENT down the stairs into the great hall of the Court in a better frame of mind than she had been in for days.

Eglantine's burst of energy had not waned. She had decided she must, for once, dress for the day, and little Nan had been summoned to pull out her prettiest morning dress and do her hair properly. Lady Mayland, on hearing the news that her daughter finally felt well enough to get out of her bed unaided, was reduced to tears of joy, and it was left to Cousin Albertine to suggest that while this was all very well, they didn't want a relapse, and that Eglantine ought to take things more slowly. Two footmen were rounded up, a divan was taken out onto the upper terrace adjoining the bedchamber, and Eglantine agreed to sit quietly in the shade, being read to, until a light nuncheon was to be served downstairs.

Polly wandered into the conservatory that ran along the side of the west wing of the Court. It was quite massive, and she had only ventured, before this, into the first few rows of familiar flowers, trying to find blooms that might cheer her cousin's sickroom.

Something more festive seemed to be in order today. She moved past the tubs of violets and marigolds, into an area filled with exotic shrubberies, where a man in a brown wool smock was sweeping up a few leaves that had fallen onto the marble flagging.

She smiled at him and turned around a corner to find her view blocked by banks of actual trees, many of which she only recognized from illustrations in the geography books of her schoolroom days.

It was another instance, she thought, of how Valremer Court tended to go too far on everything.

Many great houses might have a fine cook able to produce lavish feasts, but only at Valremer Court was that cook required to produce one every night.

Lady Sackler might import a single Floating Aromanthia, but Lord Valremer had had an entire forest brought from overseas.

There was something so very *strained* about it – as if nothing could ever be quite enough until it was too much.

She kept walking down the rows. Surely there must be more flowers – interesting, fragrant, pretty flowers that would make Eglantine feel even more cheerful and once more like herself again.

Herbs, now. Quite a long stretch of them. Well, that made sense, if one was going to insist on having a full state dinner prepared every night.

She stopped midway down the long line of foliage. Some of these were not for cooking. There was a *bella fortescue* shrub, which was supposed to be efficacious for fevers. And this – this was *runcible*, which she distinctly remembered was meant for sleeping draughts.

She looked down at the row of small plants, tucked in between a rosemary bush and another dark, green, spindly-looking thing she didn't know the name of, and her steps faltered.

"Dragon's Finger, known to produce Forgetfulness. Flesh-and-Blood, extremely dangerous, as it clouds the mind and Alters time. Oreganthea, used exclusively for Charms to force a Victim to One's Will..."

She could hear, not far away, the sound of the broom, still sweeping away.

The scent of something spicy drifted in the air. Her head swam, but she could see, in her mind's eye, the pages of a book very clearly, with its curling, tortured print and its finely-drawn pictures of all the plants that were severely proscribed by every Law, and their usage strictly forbidden.

"Miss Polly," drawled a familiar voice.

She started, guiltily.

"Admirable, is it not?" said Lord Valremer. "I trust you are finding what you seek? You must tell me if you do not!"

She opened her mouth, to say she knew not what. Her heart was pounding, and she could barely think.

There was a discreet cough behind her.

"Miss? Here's them flowers you was wanting."

Both Polly and Valremer turned. The sweeper had abandoned his broom and was holding out a rather haphazard bouquet of daisies, hollyhocks and baby's breath.

There was a moment, a very tiny moment, where she thought she might faint with relief.

"Ah," said his lordship. "Peterkin, isn't it? Very good of you to help our guest find what she needed. "

"Indeed," said Polly. Her voice was surprisingly steady. "Thank you, Peterkin."

She could feel Valremer's eyes on her, as she walked away with her flowers. She could feel them on her still, when she had regained the main house, when she was on the stairs, and even when she'd shut the door behind her in her room.

ANDREW, having nothing to report from his conversations with the gentlefolk at the Assembly, and not feeling up to facing another day of trying to eavesdrop on a parcel of country bumpkins, saddled his horse and rode out.

Not along the coast, of course. He had no wish to meet with Captain Austin and try to explain this dereliction of his assigned duties, so he turned inland with a vague thought that he might, as long as he was in the vicinity, drop in on his uncle. Indeed, his mother had written to say that it would be the decent thing to do, after all.

And, since the route there would take him past Valremer Court, or as near as made not a particle of difference, the other courteous thing would be to call and thank Mrs. Anwing for her kindnesses of the night before. And perhaps Eglantine might be about – Polly had said she was getting better, had she not?

It was not so very long before the towers of the Court came into view. Lieutenant Calthorpe was, perhaps, less impressed than the Maylands had been by the sight of them, but only because he had seen them any number of times before. The silhouette of that ancient seat did give him pause this time, though.

What, exactly, was he doing? His excuse to pay a call seemed more than a little threadbare and obvious. And what if Valremer was about? The lieutenant did not consider himself a coward, but the thought of facing his lordship in so private a situation, on his lordship's home ground, for no discernable reason other than the lovely Miss Mayland's possible presence – no. He couldn't do it.

He rode past the huge iron gates with a heavy heart. The Court was surrounded by high stone walls. Even the chance of getting a glimpse of Eglantine, always supposing she were able to walk about outdoors, was denied to him.

But a few yards on, his memories of childhood exploits surfaced. He rode a little farther and turned onto a narrow lane that led down the eastern side of the Court's vast lawns.

The walls gave way, after a distance, not to open expanses, of course, but to high hedges of holly, as impenetrable to sight as the walls had been. Here he reined in and tethered his horse. If memory served, the hedge only looked formidable. There was a way through, if he was not much mistaken, just a little bit further along.

It was more difficult than he remembered. Back then, when he'd first penetrated these confounded bushes, he'd not been so tall, and he'd had a schoolboy's disregard for his clothing. Now, forced to crouch under the overhanging thorny branches and hampered by his desire not to ruin his breeches, he found it very slow going.

The dimness under the leaves began to give way just a little. A yard or two more, he thought, and then...he froze as a strong hand clamped over his mouth and he felt a sliver of cold steel at his throat.

"Silence," whispered a raspy voice, "Make but one sound, young sir, and you will not live an instant more."

Andrew did as he was told.

There was a firm push at his back and he obeyed that unspoken order and stepped forward. They were now just an arms-length or so from where the lawn began.

"Give pledge you'll stay quiet," his captor demanded, low-voiced.

Andrew nodded. The hand came away from his mouth and, after another, interminable moment, the blade left his neck.

The man was still behind him, and he dared not turn to look, but after a pause he said softly, "Now what?"

"We wait. And watch."

Out in the brilliant sunshine, he could see a couple of men, scything the longer grass just to the south of them. He could see the house, and could just barely make out a few figures on one of the upper terraces, but they were still too far away to discern more than that.

Suddenly, he heard the sound of dogs, barking madly. Moments later, a pack of the most enormous hounds he had ever seen came bounding around the corner of the Court, baying as if they'd caught the scent of longed-for prey, and making directly for the two men tending the lawn.

The men stopped, mid- scythe-stroke, as if they'd come upon a basilisk unawares.

The baying grew louder and the dogs increased their speed, determined to run this quarry to ground.

And then, suddenly they stopped in their tracks as if invisibly leashed, still howling like wolves from the underworld, and straining against some unseen force.

A man emerged from the same direction as the hounds, sauntering casually across the green.

"Valremer," breathed Andrew.

"Aye."

His lordship stopped about halfway between the house and the dogs, and raised a hand to his lips. There was a curious, high-pitched whining sound, at which the dogs' barking cut off almost mid-yap, and then they, all of them, turned and loped back to circle around Valremer.

His lordship did not touch his dogs. He did not even seem to notice them. He was looking first at the men, who hastily went back to their work, and then, as if he sensed something else amiss, he raked his eyes along the perimeter hedges. A moment later, though, he turned away, as if satisfied with the view, and walked back the way he had come, with his dogs following mutely behind.

Andrew let out a shaky breath he hadn't realized he was holding.

"Come," said the voice, and tugged gently at Andrew's sleeve.

There was nothing to do but to follow. The man who had accosted him and held a knife to his throat was as tall as he was, but a bit more sturdily built, with broad shoulders under the rough greatcoat he wore, and he seemed to know a better route through the hedge, because it took them only a little time before they were standing in the sunshine of the lane again.

Andrew looked at his companion. He had a day or two's growth of beard, his hair ws unbrushed and a little ragged, and his clothes, well, they'd certainly seen better days. Andrew was a lieutenant and an officer of the Crown. He was a gentleman. This ruffian ought not to have had the brass to hold a knife to his throat. Or to give him orders.

And why had it seemed so natural to obey?

"You'd best be getting on, young sir."

He almost went. But then his pride asserted itself.

"What were you doing there?"

"I might ask you that question, too," said the man, grinning. "But I fancy you've the same mission as me."

"What d'you mean by that? You can't possibly –"

"I mean," said the ruffian, " that we both want to know what's going on in there, and that we've no wish to see his lordship's guests come to grief – ain't that right?"

Andrew stared at him. "Look here," he began, and then stopped and looked the man straight in the eyes. And swallowed. Hard.

"I see you aren't going to be fobbed off with mysteries," said the man, with resignation. "Well, if you won't stay out of this, I suppose we'd be better off talking this out over a pint down at the Sun."

13

I n the smaller drawing room, the joy of Eglantine's returning strength had been overwhelmed by the news from the City. Lord Mayland was left to make apologies to his host.

"I fear I must go at once," he said. "The message was very clear. My dear," he added, turning to his wife, "pray do not distress yourself. Our people say they do not believe anything was taken, and you sent the silver to the bank, did you not? The authorities wish to make sure, that is all. And I must see to repairs. It seems the thieves gained entrance by breaking a window."

"Are you certain you must go yourself?" asked Mrs. Anwing. "Surely your butler can see to hiring a glazier, and the servants must know if anything is not accounted for."

"Well, as to that, it seems they went directly for the upper rooms," said Lord Mayland. "They must have thought the ladies would leave their jewels lying about unattended, for they seem to have searched those bedchambers most thoroughly. Someone from the family must take a proper look, of course."

Polly set down her teacup very carefully. She was aware of her uncle's eyes searching her out, as if he meant, by his words, to convey something quite particular to her.

"I must go and pack directly," said Lord Mayland, after a moment. "And if you can think of anything of value you might have left behind, Polly, I pray you tell me of it now, for it seems your room was particularly disarranged."

She felt, quite distinctly, Valremer's gaze transfer to her. He had, up until now, seemed only mildly concerned by the news that the messenger from Number Four, Shalliton Place had brought. His regrets that this would take Lord Mayland away from them had been perfunctory, at best, and he had seemed as puzzled as the rest of the company by the idea that someone had chosen to break into their house while they were absent. Nothing like it had ever happened to them before.

THE NEWS OF THE BREAK-IN, coupled with the bustle that ensued as Lord Mayland took his leave, seemed to have sapped Eglantine's energies once more. Mrs. Anwing's suggestion that she return to her bed was met with only a token resistance, and since Mrs. Anwing herself took charge of her and shepherded her up the stairs with Lady Mayland trailing fretfully behind, Polly returned to the drawing room with Cousin Albertine, and, after a few minutes of awkward silence, rang for a fresh pot of tea.

The footman hesitated, looking worried.

"The thing is, miss," he said, stammering a little, "the thing is, Mrs. Anwing is very particular about the tea for upstairs. She keeps it locked up special, and right now, miss, I don't know if I ought to –"

"Don't be an idiot," said Cousin Albertine. "We can manage without these newfangled, exotic blends. A plain, ordinary pot will do very well. Honestly," she added, after the footman had nodded and gone away, "This is the most extraordinary household. I don't think much of that tea of the Anwing's, either. It tastes rather odd, and it's much too strong."

Polly said nothing. She picked up the copy of Goderet's Annual and began turning the pages, as if absorbed in contemplation of last year's summer frocks.

The tea. It seemed quite obvious to her, now.

THE AFTERNOON DRAGGED ON SLOWLY.

Polly, in an attempt to avoid his lordship, spent the greater part of it reading aloud to Eglantine from the 'Dark Lady of Gwent', while her aunt dozed on the divan.

By tea-time, Eglantine, too, was visibly flagging once more, and since her cousin could find no way to prevent anyone from drinking the fresh pot of tea brought up by little Nan (she herself managed to dump the contents of her cup into the potted aspidistra in the corner), she risked a walk in the gardens, hopeful that her host would not be lingering there.

In this she was only partially successful. She spent the first hour in blissful solitude, trying mainly to count back the days since they had arrived at Valremer Court. As nearly as she could figure, it had been the better part of three weeks since they had left the City, although another portion of her mind stubbornly resisted this accounting, certain that only a few days could have passed.

She saw, out of the corner of her eye, that Lord Valremer was down on the south lawn, talking to a rather burly man with a black watchman's cap, and turned hastily into the Long Walk that ran down to the ornamental lake that had provided so much angling pleasure to her uncle, hopeful that no one had seen her.

The shade was a welcome relief. It might be somewhat cooler here in Summersett, compared to the City, and the salty tang of the sea air was certainly invigorating, but it was still unseasonably warm, and the sun was still as relentlessly in force as ever, making any strenuous exercise unthinkable.

She made for the carved stone bench overlooking the water and sat, fanning herself with her hat and wondering about the break-in back at Number Four. Her uncle's words regarding the object of the thieves' intent had made a strong impression on her – there was, not even for an instant – any doubt in her mind what they had been looking for.

The question, of course, was why.

That the rose that Ambridge had gifted her with had been Magicked in some way was not at issue. She had known it since that awful moment in her bedchamber, when she had looked upon its darkened form.

But why anyone else should even remember the gift, let alone know how carefully she had kept it, or, still less, understand its import when she herself had not the slightest comprehension of what it could mean...that was a mystery.

"Remember me...and hold me close...for a little while..."

What on earth could he have meant by those words?

It occurred to her now that it had not been the romantic gesture everyone had assumed. He had not fixed on her in some sudden infatuation, but rather, she had been a desperate answer to an even more desperate enterprise – that somewhere in all of this, the man had tried to keep something safe, to give into her charge some terrible secret he was trying to hide, and that more than merely his life was bound up into this.

What had her maid said? Ambridge had visited here in the summer, more than once, and because of Mrs. Anwing.

Polly, although her upbringing had been as sheltered and cosseted as any of her acquaintance, was not a fool. She had heard the rumours and the sly comments – she knew, in a general way, what kind of woman Mrs. Anwing was thought to be. In anyone less-well-connected, less meshed into the web of speculation and scandal of their world, she might have been shunned by all but the more rakish and adventurous, existing only on the very fringes of Society.

So it might have only been the kind of escapade that young men were apparently so susceptible to.

Mrs. Anwing was very lovely to look at, and Polly had gathered from her months in Society that gentlemen were frequently not enormously particular about the company they kept in this regard. It was considered the part of young ladies such as herself to woo them from these kinds of low and sordid attractions, by virtue of their superior claims to goodness.

But somehow, thinking of that moment in the ballroom at Paltravers, Polly could not bring herself to believe in Ambridge's attraction to Mrs. Anwing. He had not seemed like the kind of man who could be swayed into vice so easily, and indeed, in the first weeks after she had made her curtsey, she had heard a great deal about his sterling qualities, his delightful manners, and his unbelievable virtues.

He had – he must have had – some other goal in mind.

He had entrusted a little part of his secret to her. Something in her had prompted his gift, and even if, as she rather suspected, it was only her relative unobtrusiveness and obscurity, she owed it to him not to betray that trust.

ANDREW SAT down to dine with his captain that evening with a nervous heart. He had news at last, and that must be considered an improvement, but he knew that he was treading a fine line in all directions.

"Two nights from now, you say?"

"Indeed, I am sure of it," Andrew said. "The man seemed very definite."

"A big man, you say? With a Findraisii accent?"

"As near as I could tell, sir. It sounded something like those diplomats that came to sign the treaty, anyway."

"And you're sure they said they would come in on the tide, to the place where the creek comes out below the cliffs?"

"That's what the girl said. Like she'd learnt it off by heart, too, so I don't suppose *she's* involved, in any serious way."

"Shouldn't think so. Devil of a ride, though, all the way down to Luminous Rock. Still, if we're in place before dark...the night's right for it, anyway."

"Sir?"

"No moon. It'll be true dark, you know. Nothing smugglers like better."

"I see." Andrew began to relax. The captain seemed in no way suspicious of his news, and in fact, sounded quite excited. Austin called for a second bottle, poured them each a generous glassful and offered a toast to their endeavor.

14

D espite the exertions of the previous day, Eglantine was awake and dressing when Polly looked in on her the next morning, and she was determined to join them all in the breakfast room.

"Indeed," she was saying, as Polly opened the door, "I feel quite well, Mamma. And it is so dull, seeing only these four walls."

"If you are quite certain, dearest. Only, you must not tire yourself."

"I promise I shall not."

Once in the breakfast room, she ate two slices of toast and an egg, which was, according to Cousin Albertine, more than she had managed on any other morning, although this optimistic expression was followed by the dire hope that Eglantine would not succumb to a bout of indigestion or worse.

"Nonsense," said her niece, cheerfully. "I feel perfectly well."

Mrs. Anwing looked up from the pile of correspondence that the footman had deposited beside her plate.

"Well, here is a fortunate circumstance, indeed," she said. "Lady Elias has written to ask if she might call today, with her daughters. They are all quite wild to meet you, my dear, and to see Miss Polly again, of course."

"Just the thing," said Lady Mayland, quite forgetting her worries. "Eglantine, you will want your blue morning gown. Nothing becomes you better."

Cousin Albertine sniffed. "And ten to one, she'll be in a high fever again by midnight, with all the noise and chatter and who knows who, parading in and out. "

"Oh, no, Miss Mayland." Mrs. Anwing was at her most persuasive. "We shall take every care. You must be there, too, of course. With you at her side, nothing can be amiss. Is the tea cold already, Miss Eglantine? I vow you have not taken so much as a sip."

Polly, moving over to the sideboard in search of the plum jam, looked down at the pile of letters that Mrs. Anwing had read and discarded. Two were plainly dressmaker's bills: she recognized Madame Honorine's distinctively flourishing script. On the top, though, was a mere note, a scrawl, in fact, and although she had been taught never to pry into another's private affairs, she couldn't help but take in, without the slightest effort, the few short lines there.

"Things begin to move at last, and our goal is in sight. Only keep these idiots occupied and ignorant a day or two more, and we shall have it all. Signed, H."

~

SHORTLY AFTER NOON, the Elias household turned up en masse, and in surprisingly subdued moods, having been, Polly surmised, given strict orders not to upset the recovering invalid with anything approaching high spirits.

This decorum vanished almost instantly, however, when, upon entering the drawing room, Cecily Elias (who was only fifteen) exclaimed, "Oh, how beautiful you are!", eliciting first a frown and then an indulgent smile from her mother, when she saw how easily and kindly Miss Mayland accepted the tribute. Eglantine laughed and patted the space beside her on the settee, and proceeded to make the young lady feel as if they were fast friends already.

Mr. Elias, although he had professed his ardent admiration for

Polly almost continually since the night of the Assembly, barely registered her presence. So struck was he by Eglantine's countenance that he uttered scarcely a word, but sat staring at this vision in a daze.

Tea arrived as a welcome distraction, along with a tray of tiny, jewel-like cakes. Apart from local gossip and a few remarks concerning a ball planned for the following week, there was very little that the callers had in common with their new friends, but good fortune appeared to smile on them when the door opened and two new guests were announced.

"Captain Austin, with Lieutenant Calthorpe, ma'am."

"How delightful," said Mrs. Anwing. She did not sound delighted. She sounded rather puzzled, in fact.

The effect of the announcement on Eglantine was like lightning. She sat up as straight as an arrow, and her cheeks gained a distinctly rosy hue.

"Oh," was all she said, but her expressive tone was enough to make her mother turn to study her with considerable alarm.

In this, she was not alone. Lady Elias, having watched her eldest daughter dancing with Andrew at the Assembly, had begun to form designs of her own and found herself a little put out, not least because one look at Andrew's reciprocating gaze told her all she needed to know in that quarter. Mr. Elias' stiffening lower lip indicated that he, too, had gained a fair reading of the wind's direction.

The Captain advanced into the room and made his courtesies, Andrew at his side. There was nothing out of the common, thought Polly, watching them, save for two things.

Andrew's gaze could not keep from straying towards her cousin, and that was no matter to ponder over. She might have expected it, although she wished he was not quite so obvious.

But the Captain seemed as preoccupied as his aide, in another direction. She noted that he had managed to maneuver Mrs. Anwing away from the tea-table and into a quieter part of the room, their heads close together in low-voiced conversation.

Well, if that was where the woman's interest lay, so much the better, although it did not, for all its intimacy, have quite the feel of two lovers enjoying a little private speech.

What was surprising was Cousin Albertine, who might have been expected to have joined with Lady Mayland in thwarting Eglantine's obvious desire to engage Lieutenant Calthorpe's attention, since his station in life, while respectable, was in no way the starry firmament that a Mayland heiress and this Season's reigning Toast might be thought to command, seemed oblivious to this new development.

Instead, she had, by sheer bluntness and an imperious disregard for ordinary manners, engaged both Lady Mayland and Lady Elias in an examination of some shrubberies planted just below the farthest windows of the room, plying them both with questions about their origins and care that were inexplicable and obtuse.

By the time anyone with any power to re-order these arrangements was even aware of it, young Cecily had been supplanted on the settee, and Andrew and Eglantine, although not strictly speaking behaving in any way improperly, were having a wordless conversation all their own, and seeming to shut out everyone else present.

There was, in the midst of this, a rather awkward pause.

"This room is so pretty," said Polly, in a gallant attempt to recover some civility.

"It's even prettier in early summer. Isn't it, Felicia?" Cecily said, appealing to her older sister for confirmation.

"Indeed. It gets the evening sun, then. But I daresay you will see that for yourself, someday, will you not, Miss Mayland?"

"Oh," This appeal to Eglantine seemed to catch her off-guard. "Oh, I should not think – that is, I cannot see..."

"Were you here in summer?" The words were out of Polly's mouth before she could help herself.

"Oh, yes! I was only just out, you know, so Mamma and I came to call. And it turned out it was not quite the thing, for the Duke of Ambridge was visiting. It was very odd, since I'm sure we had no notion of his being here. But he was very pleasant to us. So very sad we were, to hear...But I expect you know more about that than I."

"Indeed, I do not," Polly said, faintly.

"We heard it was a wasting sickness, is that not right, Mamma? He seemed very well when we met him, although a little pale and listless, and his attention did seem to wander somewhat. But then, when he left, we heard that he went up north to hunt, or some such, and then on into the City, and everything seemed well enough. And then – so shocking, when a young man is so unexpectedly and suddenly struck down."

"Indeed, it was excessively sad," said Mrs. Anwing, tonelessly. She and the Captain had edged back toward the group around the settee. "One feels most sincerely for his family."

"Felicia, you must not gossip," said Lady Elias, turning back from the windows. "It was very tragic, but I am persuaded that we must not dwell on such unhappiness. There is the new duke, and I am sure he must do very well. I expect the lieutenant can support me on this, since he must be well-acquainted with him."

"I?" said Andrew, with some surprise. "Indeed, I am not. Ambridge was part of the occupying force in Fendrais, you know, right up until his brother's demise. The news was slow getting to him, too, they say, for he nearly missed the funeral. He cashed out his commission directly, or so I heard, and has been little minded to gad about in the City since."

"So you have never met him?" Mrs. Anwing

"I believe I saw him from a distance, once, just after joining the regiment. Beyond that, ma'am, he is an utter stranger."

Polly looked at Andrew sharply. While she could not have said she was like a sister to him, she reckoned that she knew him fairly well – well enough to be certain, at that moment, that he was, if not telling an outright lie, engaging in a prevarication.

"He has kept himself to himself," agreed Mrs. Anwing. "Other than Lord Valremer, I believe none of us have ever encountered him, being younger than his brother, and going directly into the army so young."

Lady Mayland turned from her vague perusal of the shrubbery.

"I believe Lord Mayland met him, once," she remarked. "In Samaris, after the Armistice was signed. A bit of a tearaway, he said."

Captain Austin, raising his tea cup to his lips at that exact moment, was seized with a sudden fit of coughing.

In the ensuing attempts to calm this ailment, the status of the current duke of Ambridge was forgotten, and when more general discourse resumed, the ladies began to form a plan for an excursion to show the Misses Mayland the Summerpoole Castle ruins, which were a very famous and picturesque attraction for visitors.

15

On the following morning, the small company of Excise-men rode out from the town.

Since Captain Austin was convinced that nearly every person dwelling within a mile of Summerpoole was engaged in some way in the smuggling ring, they rode first towards the north, as if they were going onto the Downs for their regular drills.

Once there, however, they did not stop, but circled back towards the south by way of Rambler's Drift, where the sergeant had made arrangements for the day's provisions, and by late afternoon, they were already carefully concealed above a little ravine below Luminous Rock, from which vantage point they could see both the headlands and the beach, and were ideally placed to apprehend their quarry.

～

THE DINNER SERVED to Valremer's guests that evening was, if anything, more spectacular than any before.

There was, in addition to a saddle of venison dressed in a White Sauce, some medallions of beef, as well as an entire Salmon encrusted with rose-coloured salt and crowned with preserved lemons.

The Sallat course included not only the usual herbs and lettuces, but adorable posies constructed from asparagus spears and edible flowers, arranged in delicate pastry vases on their plates, as if they had just come straight from the gardens.

The jellies and sweetmeats were presented on an enormous silver salver, lined with real lace, instead of the cut-parchment imitations usually reserved for these purposes, and they glowed like gemstones in the light of the enormous chandelier overhead.

Valremer was at his most urbane. He listened in apparent fascination to Lady Mayland's account of not only the expense of sending all of the family silver to the bank, but to her description of several of the most important pieces, all the while pressing his guests to try this dish or that, and attempting to convince Cousin Albertine to drink a glass of elderberry wine for her health.

Afterwards, he announced that without Lord Mayland there to share his port, he was of a mind to dispense with convention and join the ladies in the drawing room immediately, and, having done so, proceeded to charm Lady Mayland by suggesting they play piquet.

On the surface, it seemed an unexceptional evening.

And yet...

There was something wrong. Polly could feel it.

It was not merely Valremer's mood. He seemed always to have been capable of somehow putting them at ease when he chose, despite his reputation for set-downs and occasional rudenesses, not to mention his propensity for malignant flirtation.

Tonight, he was not merely in good spirits, but almost excited. In general, his lordship tended to short, pithy remarks, delivered in a deliberately slow drawl, but tonight he seemed uncharacteristically loquacious, indeed, positively eager to fill every silence, and there was a slight flush to his cheeks.

On the other hand, Mrs. Anwing seemed subdued and distracted.

For once, she left Polly and Eglantine to themselves, and busied herself at the little escritoire in the corner, where she claimed to be catching up on her correspondence. Her writing things were out, to be sure, but if any letter was completed, Polly saw no evidence of it.

Instead, their hostess spent a good deal of time looking out the window beside her, checking the ormolu clock on the shelf above the desk, and several times getting up to just "check on the servants" or some other errand, leaving the room for long minutes at a time.

At half-past nine, Cousin Albertine announced that she was retiring, in accents that suggested anyone who remained behind her in the drawing room was committing the most grievous of social sins, and but for Lady Mayland, who had managed to win a very pretty sum from his lordship, the rest of the party greeted this veiled stricture with relief.

OUT ON THE BEACH, Captain Austin was unleashing a heretofore unsuspected vocabulary of invective at the universe.

THE MEN IN UNIFORM STOOD, bewildered and annoyed. Andrew was – well, he would not say "frightened", but he was, to say the least, uneasy. The ruse had served, but he devoutly wished himself otherwhere, for it had occurred to him that his own position in this was precarious, at best. At any moment, the captain might consider where this spurious and embarrassing adventure's genesis lay.

THE MEN in ordinary workmen's clothes were merely amused.

THE EXCISEMEN HAD WATCHED in anticipation as the little boat had rowed ashore. They'd waited patiently, watching as the three men aboard had shifted the wicker creels onto the shingle.

They'd then marched out to arrest the smugglers, only to find that the creels contained no contraband, but a mess of freshly-caught herring.

~

SHE COULD NOT SLEEP. Something about the evening air – so close and oppressive! – kept Polly restless and half-awake, twice tossing aside the coverlet and getting out of bed to splash her face with cool water from the basin on the dressing table.

She had been well-served, she owned, for introducing the subject of summer, which had brought the late Duke of Ambridge into the conversation. The results might have been predictable, since every other mention of the man had unsettled her peace of mind so extremely. She could not think of what she had been about, save that her curiosity about his visits to Valremer had exerted a powerful hold upon her mind. The desire to unlock this riddle, if riddle it was and not merely an indiscreet affair, was fast gaining the status of an obsession.

Why should he have come here – and so frequently, too, if little Nan was to be believed – if it was not for the lures cast out by the Anwing?

There was something so odd about it all, and then his untimely demise - she was convinced now that these two things were not unconnected. But how?

There was something she could almost catch hold of. A stray thought kept tugging just at the edges of her mind, something that had almost made its way into her thoughts when Felicity Elias had talked about the Duke's death, that she was suddenly quite sure was the key to the thing, if only she could bring to mind just what it was. She frowned, trying to remember what had caught her attention, but just as she began to relive the conversation in her mind, there occurred several things, all at once, that disrupted her train of thought.

There was first of all, the baying of the hounds.

She sat up in a panic, for they sounded quite near. From the very start, the presence of those enormous and ferocious-seeming beasts had upset her, but over the course of their stay here, they had seen precious little of them, and heard even less, and she had, on some level, put their existence out of her mind.

Now, the howls were altogether too real, and her lively imagination conjured up a vision of them, slavering and out-of-control, bent on rending some hapless and unwitting trespasser to bits.

Before she could be completely overset by this image, she heard a faint, yet insistent tapping at the long windows beside the armoire. It was feeble enough that she immediately assumed that she had imagined it, but a moment later, the sound came again.

"Miss?" said a man's voice, in a hopeful tone. "Miss? I do beg of you..."

She slipped from her bed without thought, and moved to the windows. They had been left open, just a little, in hopes of cooler, night-time breezes to aid her sleep, and in the moonlight, she saw that the gardener's assistant, young Peterkin, was standing outside on the upper terrace.

And beyond him stood a taller, bigger man, his face still in shadow.

"Please, miss, if you could help us?"

In any other situation, she might have hesitated. Indeed, she did hesitate, but the memory of Valremer's acute and penetrating gaze, and his coldly calculating demeanor in the conservatory, rose up in her mind's eye. Peterkin had done her a signal service, without any prompting, and before she could even begin to consider the gross impropriety of the thing, she had pushed the window open wide and beckoned.

Only the tall man climbed over the low sill. Peterkin, with a sigh of relief, had stepped back, muttering, "I'll manage them dogs, Jack," before melting away into the night.

And before either she or her unknown guest could exchange a word, there was the sound of a commotion in the hallway outside. There were footsteps, shouted commands, and the sound of doors slamming.

And then a peremptory knock at her own door.

The man looked at her.

Polly cast her eyes wildly around the room.

"Miss Polyantha!" Lord Valremer's voice was commanding.

The man turned toward the armoire.

"Don't be an idiot," hissed his rescuer. "It's the first place they'll look!"

There was another knock at the door. Louder, this time.

"Miss Polyantha," said Valremer, in a tone that suggested he was trying not to shout. "Are you awake?"

"I – I – oh, what is it, my lord?" Her voice trembled.

She moved to the bed. It was a massive thing, all carved oak and brocade hangings – positively medieval – and in addition to the mound of pillows that decorated it, it boasted a velvet bolster running the entire width of the ornate headboard. Polly pulled it back and motioned frantically at her intruder.

"There's has been – at least, we think there has been an incident. I must come in and see that you are -"

"That you will not do, sir!" That was Cousin Albertine. She sounded even more out of temper than usual. "Such goings-on! Waking up an entire household in the middle of the night!"

Her visitor grinned back at Polly with appreciation, and climbed into the space she had opened up. She shoved the bolster back against him, flung the pillows over the long cushion, and without a second thought, climbed back into the bed and pulled the covers over herself.

"Miss Mayland," said his lordship, "You must understand – we must make certain the miscreant has not found his way into the house! I merely wish to be sure that –"

"My lord!" This time, the elderly Miss Mayland was truly scandalized. "Do I understand you? You intend to force your way into a young lady's bedchamber?"

"No! That is, yes. But only to –"

"Are you mad? You shall not. This is unconscionable."

"But surely you see that we must make sure..." Polly could only imagine the look on Cousin Albertine's face, as Valremer's voice trailed away in a thoroughly unaccustomed uncertainty.

"I," announced his adversary, "I shall go in to my niece's room myself, and ascertain her safety, my lord, and you shall wait outside. Polly, do not be alarmed."

The door handle turned.

Cousin Albertine en déshabillé was a truly magnificent sight.

Her grey hair was done up into a vast mound of rag-curlers that increased the size of her head by at least a third. She had surmounted this arrangement with a beribboned linen mobcap that looked rather like a gigantic, lacy footstool.

Over her nightdress, she wore, in addition to a padded brown silk wrapper, two long, dark-coloured shawls, draped, Polly surmised, to obscure any remnant or lingering suggestion of the female figure, and her feel were clad in rather startlingly bright and ornately embroidered slippers.

Polly, mindful of her manners, tried not to stare at this apparition.

Her cousin looked her over, then cast her eyes around the room.

"Seen anyone?" It appeared that Cousin Albertine had a heretofore unsuspected sense of humour. Her tone was decidedly satirical.

Polly shook her head. Her cousin moved to the window and called out, "No one hiding behind the curtains, my lord."

She bent, stiffly, and lifted the brocaded bedskirt.

"Nor under the bed."

The armoire doors were opened, then closed again. She turned back to Polly and looked at her searchingly for a moment, and then, shockingly, she smiled, winked, and walked out, shutting the door firmly behind her.

For quite an entire minute, Polly found she could not move. Her heart was still pounding, but little by little, her breathing slowed again, and she began to believe that she was, in fact, safe once more. She listened as the commotion in the corridor receded, and then faded away completely.

Then she hopped back out of the bed, ran to the door, and firmly turned the key in the lock with a satisfying click.

When she looked back at her bed, the intruder had pushed aside the pillows and the bolster to free himself.

"That was powerful kind of you, Miss," he said. "Resourceful, too! I wouldna' have given thought to it, meself."

She glared at him, for his tone was not grateful, at all. In point of fact, he seemed almost to be mocking her.

"I doubt you have seen many bedchambers in houses like these," she said, coldly.

"You might be surprised, Miss."

"I suppose," Polly said, ironically, "that you are invited everywhere."

"Well, not so seldom as ye'd think, love."

He turned his back, and crossed the room to stand in front of the armoire,

"Is this where fine ladies keep their treasures?" he asked.

"That depends," Polly said. There was something about this ruffian that was more than unsettling. Why on earth had she let him into her room?

"On what?" He opened the armoire doors and appeared to be entranced by the row of delicate evening gowns arrayed therein.

"The lady. Or the treasure, I suppose."

"And what treasures d'ye keep, Miss Polly?" He turned back to her. "A king's ransom in gold? A secret recipe for the nectar of the gods? Wait – I have it: the love letters from your spurned beaux!"

This was, for Polly, an arrow too close to the mark. She felt her face grow hot, and her grip on her temper slipped.

"Do you mean to rob me of my few trinkets, as your thank-you? I might have expected it, I suppose, from such as you!"

"Indeed, you might," he agreed, grinning back at her. "But I have no use for a lady's jewels, be they never so fine. My tastes run otherwhere."

At this, Polly became suddenly aware that she was standing barefoot, clad only in her thin cambric nightdress, in the middle of the night, with a strange man whose name she could not remember.

Before she could even think to back away or reach for her robe, he had closed the distance between them, enfolding her in a rough embrace, and she found herself being quite ruthlessly kissed.

It lasted only a moment – a moment that seemed an eternity to Polly. But almost as soon as it had begun, it ended.

A voice from the darkness outside whispered, urgently, "Jack? Jack, ye must be away. I've drawn off the dogs, but it weren't be long before they're on us agin!"

He had already let her go. He was already at the windows.

He was gone.

Polly stood stock-still in the middle of the room, her hand on her mouth, frozen in what she assured herself was a state of icy rage.

16

Between the oppressive heat and the night-time alarms, it seemed that no one in Valremer Court had slept well.

It was nearly half-past Morning Bells before Nan crept into Polly's room with the tea-tray, and when Lady Mayland finally was roused enough to put in an appearance in the breakfast room, she found her niece alone, staring listlessly at a plate of bacon and eggs that sat cooling before her.

"Polly, my love, you look so pale! Are you unwell?"

Polly looked up, rather blankly. "I think I have a head-ache coming on."

"And no wonder," said her aunt. "I vow, this weather is enough to make anyone blue-devilled. Even Cousin Albertine is laid low today. Your uncle would say it is the sciatica, but I think she is merely cross, because the dogs woke her."

Polly gave her a tremulous smile.

"You should take some fresh air," said Lady Mayland, illogically. "Perhaps that will put the colour back into your cheeks."

Polly did not answer. She did not need to. Mrs. Anwing bustled into the room, looking quite furious, and not the least concerned with anyone else's preoccupations. This was a fleeting glimpse, however. Upon seeing the two ladies, she smoothed away her angry expression, and directed a gaze of spurious benevolence at her guests.

"Miss Polly, I have been looking everywhere for you! Indeed, I had supposed you already out and about, since the day is so fine." Here, she paused and looked the young lady over. "I wonder if you might do me a small service? I would not ask, but the household is so much at sixes and sevens, what with all the excitement last night! I declare, servants are all alike: one tiny upset, and they act as if the entire world has come undone. So much to put to rights today – I do not know if I am coming or going."

Not for nothing had Lady Mayland engaged a first-rate governess and overseen that gentlewoman's teaching with an exacting eye. Polly, without a moment's hesitation, responded as any young lady and a guest must do.

"But, of course, ma'am. If there is anything I can assist you with, I am at your service."

"It's the merest nothing, to be sure. But there are some things in the town that need to be seen to, and I cannot spare anyone just now. If you could take charge of my little commissions, I could order John to bring out the gig for you. And Summerpoole is very lively on market days – it might be an entertaining outing for you!"

"Just the thing," said Lady Mayland. "Do you know, Mrs. Anwing, I was just telling Polly she might wish to be outside and doing, to bring her out of the dismals. But can you spare a maid to accompany her, with all this upset?"

"Oh, there need not be the slightest concern for that. This is not the City, after all. She will be perfectly safe on her own. But it must be Miss Polly's choice, of course."

"Naturally, I will go," Polly said. It occurred to her that Lady Mayland was not wrong, in fact. To be away from here, alone and away from the heavy weight of the Court: it was like a burden on her spirit, and one that seemed to slow her thoughts to a crawl. To have silence, and time to think – how she longed for that.

"Splendid. John Coachman can set you down at the Sun and wait for you there, and I will write out exactly the places you may go, and what to collect. And the Pink Bells is a most respectable tea-room: they will give you a nuncheon, if you like. Merely say that it is at *my* wish, and I promise, they will take every care of you!"

~

LITTLE NAN WAS SERIOUSLY WORRIED.

She was aware that her occasional employment at the Court had more to do with her habit of silence in the face of the Court's formidable owner and his equally formidable cousin, than in any other quality she might possess. Mrs. Anwing did not tolerate idle chatter, or clumsiness, or even any tiny departure from innocuous and unobjectionable physical appearance. One could not be too plain, but neither could one be too pretty, nor slow-witted, nor clever: in fact, one needed to be, in public at least, as near to invisible as was possible without the gift of Magick.

Nan fit that bill almost perfectly. She was more or less tongue-tied in the master's presence, and nearly so when Mrs. Anwing deigned to notice her; she was small and deft in her movements, and intelligent enough to remember and follow any instruction given to the letter, unlike her friend Dolly. Dolly was not merely outspoken, but loudly rebellious, when orders that struck her as pointless or foolish were handed down.

Dolly couldn't help it, of course. Her old gramps was one of those cantankerous sorts, always railing about the gentry and their wicked ways. Nan could sympathize – she'd seen enough, working those infrequent days up at the Court, to agree with him. But she liked the coin it brought in, and she could not see how holding her tongue and earning it in any way stopped her from thinking so little of the people who handed it to her.

"What the eyes don't see, the mind don't object to." That's what her mam always said, and it was true. Mrs. Anwing wasn't to know that her name, belowstairs, was one spoken with heavy sarcasm, or that they thought her impudent and encroaching. No better than any of them, she was, what with her mother having been a housekeeper who had entrapped an old widower into marriage, and her daughter doing much the same, years later.

The lord, though...that was a different matter. Him she tried not to think on at all, with his cold eyes, and his murderous dogs. He had never noticed her, not in any particular way, and for that, she was grateful. She'd heard some things about people he did notice.

But today as she walked into the third-best guest chamber in the west wing of Valremer Court, in order to retrieve the morning tea tray, she stopped in dismay.

His lordship was standing in the centre of the room, and surveying it all with a critical eye, but as she entered, he swung around to fix that narrow gaze on her.

"Ah. Nan," he said. There was a note of indefinable menace in that voice. She swallowed nervously and bobbed what she hoped was a suitably respectful curtsey. How did he

even know her name? She had hoped she had never before come to even that much of his attention.

"Sir," she whispered, eyes downcast.

"I was looking at the window latches," he said. "After last night, I wished to be sure our guests are perfectly safe."

"Just so, sir."

"Carry on, then," he said, and stalked past her into the corridor, shutting the door behind him.

It was quite a moment or two before Nan could breathe properly again.

It was very upsetting, but it was also curious. Why should he have wished to explain himself to her, of all people? It was his house, after all, and he was Quality, free to do whatever he wished. In her experience, not very much that the gentry did made any sense, but she rarely questioned this. Those with both wealth and Powers were a mystery and then some, and they but rarely deigned to acknowledge lesser mortals' existence, let alone justify their actions to those not equal to them.

She picked up the tea tray and cast her eyes around the room, making sure that all was as it ought to be – Mrs. Anwing had made a long and repetitive speech about the courtesies they must show Valremer's guests.

There was a dark grey scrap of something on the carpet. She set the tray down again and bent to look.

Just a bit of...flower? A rose petal, but of no colour she had ever seen in nature. She stood, petal in hand, and glanced around the room. There was nothing like it anywhere: the only flowers here were some orangey-red chrysanthemums set in a tall crystal vase on the dressing-table. But that was on the far side of the room and...

The armoire door. It was open, just a little bit. Surely it had been well-latched, after she'd laid out Miss Polly's walking dress? She was sure of it, because she distinctly remembered the metallic sound it had made when she had closed it.

Nan looked down and saw that the drawer at the foot of the armoire was open, too, just the merest crack, and that, she was even more positive, had been shut tight, because she had been very careful about putting away Miss Polly's gloves and necklet the night before. Miss Polly didn't have many jewels, and Nan had guessed that they were precious to her. Besides, she liked Miss Polly.

She shut the drawer very firmly. She closed the armoire door and made sure the latch was fast. Then she picked up the tea tray again, and left the room, her smooth brow now furrowed with concentration.

THE TOWN, as Mrs. Anwing had predicted, was bustling with people.

In the open square in front of the Golden Sun, there was, in addition to the row of makeshift booths filled with vegetables, a set of wicker pens housing all the sheep and chickens, and the air was loud with voices as local farmers haggled with each other over prices and quality.

Polly was grateful that Mrs. Anwing's errands took her almost immediately away from all this clamor, leading her first down a wide thoroughfare at the south end of the green towards the glover's establishment, and from there to a small, dimly-lit shop filled with jars of herbs. Here, she was given a chair and a dish of tea while she waited for the list of foreign spices required to be weighed out, wrapped in twists of brown paper, and tucked into her basket.

Mrs. Anwing's list had included a very definite itinerary for her errands, in fact, along with clearly written directions.

"There's no sense in you wandering aimlessly about," her hostess had remarked, when handing her the two sheets of creamy writing paper inscribed with these instructions and reeking of some spice-laden perfume. "This will make it the easiest thing in the world, and will fetch you up at the Bells at the end. You may send for John to collect you there whenever you wish!"

And she had not been wrong in supposing Polly would find much to entertain her on her excursion. Summerpoole might not be the City, but it was lively enough, after so many quiet days, to give any young woman a variety of distractions. In addition to the amusement of watching a man quite literally arguing with his pig and then hauling that squealing animal towards the square, she had come upon a bookstall. Stopping to examine the volumes of poetry, she had discovered a copy of her father's very first foray into print. It wasn't his best, but it was still considered a classic, and one no aspiring versifier ever neglected to study. Unlike the more common, leather-bound versions, this one had been covered in deep blue velvet, with delicately embroidered vines and flowers along the spine, and she spent several minutes admiring the workmanship.

At the hat shop, she encountered Felicity Elias and her mother examining some new styles, and was immediately enlisted as an Arbiter of Fashion in aiding their choices. Here, she gained Lady Elias' eternal gratitude by persuading Felicity that the bottle-green velvet turban was not, in fact, what any young woman of Taste would choose.

"And in this heat, too, you know, you would be swooning in a trice," Polly had added, as a clincher to her argument, and this, if nothing else, had convinced Miss Elias that perhaps the dainty straw bonnet trimmed with lace was, after all, much more the thing.

She was nearly done. According to her list, she needed only to find the butcher that supplied Valremer Court with its never-ending stream of beeves and legs of mutton, and make sure that the next week's menu was provided for. She need not, Mrs. Anwing had assured her, take charge of a single item there, for it was always arranged with the shopkeeper that the meats would be delivered each day.

She stood on the pavement, studying her instructions carefully. The butcher's shop appeared to be some distance from the other places she had been directed to. It was not to be wondered at, of course, since enterprises like these tended to be somewhat noisome and not generally permitted in the vicinity where even the modestly well-to-do had homes.

She started down the avenue, admiring the objects displayed in the windows of a shop selling porcelain tea wares, and strolled into the narrower street leading west.

The ever-increasing heat of the afternoon was becoming more intense. Halfway down the street, she turned almost gratefully into the little lane her directions advised, for the closeness of the build-ings promised some shade, at least, and she needed that relief. Indeed, she was becoming quite light-headed.

She turned again, and then turned once more, and found herself in a shabby-looking side road. It was almost deserted, and she could see no signs announcing any sort of enterprise or storefront. There was nothing and no one here, except for a couple of raggedy boys playing at some game in the rubbish-strewn gutter.

This could not be right.

She reread her instructions. Perhaps she had turned too soon, and Mrs. Anwing had meant something else? It was so hot – it would be no wonder if she had misread, for she was feeling quite faint.

She walked back up to the last junction, surveyed the road in both directions, and consulted the notes once more. No, the words were clear enough. At least, she thought so: it was hard to read, or even to think, when the air seemed so close and suffocating. She looked at the papers again. Her destination must be there, and she simply had not observed it.

Polly retraced her steps, and began to walk, holding her skirts carefully, down past the children.

There was, incongruously, the sound of carriage wheels, rumbling behind her along the alley. Polly turned her head almost absently to look at this, vaguely aware that the street was really far too narrow for any such conveyance to navigate it with safety.

It was only afterward that she realized that there had been footsteps behind her, even, perhaps, a smothered exclamation, and then, as if in a dream, she experienced a sudden rush of vertigo, a swooning sensation, and the feeling of small hands pushing her, as the world reeled over and she began to tumble forward, into the path of that oncoming coach.

There was no time to even cry out – she could almost feel the horses' hooves and the carriage wheels upon her, hear the sound of her bones breaking – and then, inches from the cobbles, a powerful force pulled her, decisively and without gentleness, back from that brink.

The coach rolled by in a blur of colour and clatter.

She felt herself deposited roughly onto the pavement. A deep and familiar voice said "Are you all right, Polly?" but she couldn't respond. Her vision blurred - she couldn't see anything clearly at all. Her heart was pounding, and she was shaking so very hard.

She turned her face into the rough woolen greatcoat of the man who held her, and wept.

She was aware, later, that they must have walked, and some distance, too, but at the time, she only knew that he was holding her close, and that he was talking in a low, reassuring voice, telling her the one thing she already knew: that she was safe, love, she was, and that all was well. She remembered nothing else until she found herself sitting in a cool, dark kitchen in some house she did not recognize, and a cheerful, motherly-looking woman was setting a chipped, white pottery mug down on the pine table in front of her.

Behind her, she could hear Jack, in a low voice, giving orders to someone, and then a door shut quietly, and they were alone.

17

He was sitting across from her, studying her as if he had never seen her before. She lifted the mug to her lips, and gazed back at him. He had, she noted, a thin, pale scar across one corner of his forehead.

In the novels she had read, scars were said to be quite dashing.

She had not, as a rule, ever believed this, but apparently, it was true after all. She found herself thinking that if any of the gentlemen she had stood up with during the balls and cotillions she had so far experienced had looked anything like her rescuer, she might well have lost her heart a score of times.

The tea was very sweet and milky, and not at all how she normally liked it. Yet it was strangely comforting, even as the silence stretched out between them.

"I – I must thank you, of course," Polly said, eventually.

"Indeed, you need not. After all, you did the same for me, more or less."

"I did not do that for you, though."

"Why did you, then?"

"Peterkin – he – well, he did not deserve to lose his place for your crimes, did he?"

"You've a kind heart," he said. "But the world will likely cure you of it, soon enough."

"That is very cynical, do you not think?"

"It'll be the way of things, that's all. Knowledge has its price." He smiled. It was not a very nice smile. It was mocking and unkind. "As you'll have already discovered, I am sure."

She thought, belatedly, not only of his impossible impertinence of the night before, but, suddenly, of her instinctive trust, and her fingers clinging to the lapels of his coat. Colour flooded her cheeks.

"What I do not understand," she said, trying desperately to regain her composure, "is how you came to be there at all!"

He made no answer to this. She looked at that coat, now draped over the settee in the corner, and felt suddenly, unaccountably, cold.

"You've been watching me."

"Say, rather, that I have been watching his lordship, and those he watches," Jack said.

"But why? What has he to do with you?"

"Ah. A tangled tale, m'dear, and not one easily unraveled. But drink your tea. We must get you to some place where you can call for a carriage, and in a reasonable time, too."

"The Pink Bells," Polly said, mechanically. "I was to send for the coachman from there."

He nodded.

"I still wish to know what it is that concerns you about this," Polly said. "And why you should always be where I am. For you have been, several times. You were in Shalliton Place, weeks ago. Don't deny it. I remember it perfectly."

"And if I say you are mistaken?"

"I would not believe you," she said, with asperity. "I know what my eyes see, sir. If I were a more suspicious person, I might name you a 'filching-cove', and say that you will end on the gallows!"

To her surprise, he burst out laughing.

"How do you even come to know words like that, Polly? I doubt you learned them in the schoolroom."

"Does the shoe not fit? For you must know, we were burgled, not six nights past, and my uncle was forced to return to the City because of it."

"I would not pin too much importance on that, love," he began, but just then, the door opened, and a young man slipped into the room. "Ah. Here is your escort at last. You must go now, and quickly, too, before anyone becomes anxious about you."

Out in the street, she saw that the afternoon was waning. The boy stood a little way off, waiting for her.

"Young Tompkin here will take you as far as the Bells, and then run back to the Golden Sun to give your message." He handed her the market-basket.

Polly nodded. Her bad temper had vanished with the prospect of returning to Valremer Court. Only now did she grasp the magnitude of what had happened, and what he had saved her from.

"Jack," she said. Her voice shook. "Jack, I am sorry. I never thanked you properly, and I should have done so. And I very much fear..." Her voice trailed away. Even now, it seemed preposterous.

"Do not fret overmuch. I do not think - that is, I am almost certain that - well, have a care to yourself, that is all." He took her hand. "Good-bye, my dear."

His voice was firm, as if to tell her that her lapses in both judgment and tact were now safely past and buried. It had the ring of finality.

It ought to have comforted her.

It did not.

"Yes. Of course. I do wish you well."

"Filching-cove that I am? That is handsome of you, indeed." He sounded amused. "Tompkin, be sure to avoid the Dartmund Road. Miss Polly does not need to be quizzed by every bumpkin in the world."

MRS. ANWING WATCHED with chagrin as her cousin counted out the gold coins and handed them over to the man he'd hired. She had said nothing, so far, even when the man had arrived with the two boys in tow, and with the very worst of news.

The man swore, even now, that he had done exactly as Valremer had instructed, even repeating the words he had been made to memorize so perfectly, and he maintained he had seen no one but his boys on the street, not a one, until he'd looked back after he'd passed the girl and was barreling away as fast as he could.

She had thought the plan unwise from the very outset, but Valremer had been in a cold fury since the night of the opera, and nothing she had said had seemed even to register with him.

He had been almost to the end of some elegantly surreptitious binding charm, twice now, a charm that would have made Eglantine his own in a most untraceable way, and each time, her dratted cousin had come crashing in upon his plans and spoiled the thing.

Even today, when their goal was certain, nothing could have turned him from his course. Miss Polyantha could not be allowed to go unpunished.

But it had not served. The chit had the devil's own luck, to be sure, and so had had the late Duke of Ambridge, Powers rot him. How he had hoodwinked them! And what a sly minx the Mayland girl had turned out to be. Even Mrs. Anwing had not grasped the significance of that careless compliment the late duke had bestowed, until almost too late.

The man in the black cap left, smirking, with the two boys falling in step as he went, and they heard the green baize door leading to backstairs, slamming shut behind them.

Valremer slumped back into his chair.

"Well," she said, finally, "one hopes he will keep his tongue between his teeth, at any rate."

"Oh, he'll not speak. You may be assured he knows me well enough for that."

It was almost impossible not to ask him whatever had possessed him. Trying to murder a young girl, in broad daylight – and for what? They had the glyph, now, and while the timing might not be perfect, the ritual would surely still gain them all their desires. Even more surely, there was nothing Miss Polyantha Mayland could possibly know, or even suspect, that could harm them.

And long odds they were, even if she did. What could she say, and to whom, that would be in any way believable?

POLLY'S RETURN to Valremer Court, despite the lateness of the hour, occasioned very little comment. Not even her fumbling excuses as to why she had not, after all, managed to convey Mrs. Anwing's instructions to the butcher gave rise to any questioning. Mrs. Anwing merely looked at her rather oddly, and then said only that, to be sure, it was no great matter, and that she would send someone into town on the morrow.

Lady Mayland seemed unaware of her niece's tardiness, too, since she had spent the afternoon napping on a divan in her daughter's chamber, and it was left to Cousin Albertine to remark on the poor manners it would show if Polly did not instantly repair to her room and begin dressing for dinner, but since no one else had even begun to think of doing so, Polly found this more amusing than not.

Still, it afforded her the excuse she needed to disappear upstairs and make an attempt, however poor it might be, to compose herself for another long evening in the company of at least two people she now felt even more strongly she could not trust.

18

I t was not the most pleasant evening.

The ever-present heat did not abate at sundown and none of the ladies even attempted so much as a gauze shawl, nor would there have been any need to dampen their gowns, had any of them had any wish to discreetly flout convention and show off their charms more fully. Even Cousin Albertine came down to the dining-room with bare arms and flushed cheeks, and with a scented handkerchief at the ready.

It was entirely possible, Polly thought, that the heat accounted for the lack of appetite exhibited. Mrs. Anwing merely picked at the delicacies on her plate, and Lord Valremer raised his quizzing glass at the roasted leg of lamb on offer, and coldly declined it.

Even Lady Mayland seemed aware of the tension in the room and cast imploring glances at Polly and Eglantine, wordlessly begging them to keep the conversation from flagging, but to no avail. Eglantine, despite her protests to the contrary, seemed to have sunk once more into a languid and exhausted state, and Cousin Albertine, too, was unusually silent.

Once released from the table, as Mrs. Anwing rose with a nervous smile on her face and led the ladies out, Polly murmured that she needed a new book to read, and escaped to the quiet of the library.

It wasn't, she thought, so much that she needed distraction, although that would have been welcome, if she could have found it. It was, rather, that she could feel her terror mounting. Who else could have known exactly where she would have been, and chosen the timing so neatly, but the Anwing? And why?

She had been pacing the room, but now she stopped and stared at the crowded shelves, loaded with handsomely bound volumes of "The Histories", without much interest. The shelf above contained various collections of poetry, her father's works as well as the many other acclaimed versifiers down through the ages.

And above those? She squinted up at them. Mostly, they seemed to be old songbooks. Cousin Albertine might enjoy them: she liked to reminisce about how much better the music of her girlhood was when compared with "modern" melodies.

At the end of that topmost shelf, she saw a title that, oddly enough, she recognized.

It was that same tedious book the librarian had insisted she take. But it was not the small, shabby copy that she had been given.

This copy was plainly but expertly bound in soft, shiny leather, and it was altogether larger and thicker than the book she had been given.

She had to stand on tiptoes, and even then, she could only just manage to slide the book out from the shelf by hooking one finger under the bottom of its spine. But slide forward it did, and then so easily that it very nearly dropped onto the floor – she only barely managed to catch it.

The tome fell open in her hands, as if by long custom and usage, to a page she knew instantly was not one included in her version.

"To Live Long and Full Through Darker Means" – the deep black flourishes of an old-fashioned typescript flowed across the top of the right-hand page.

∾

PETERKIN HAD HAD A RATHER TRYING day.

For one thing, there was the fact that he had not gotten much sleep.

Then there was a series of inscrutable lectures delivered, first by That Woman, and then repeated, in various ways, by both Mr. Jenkins and Mrs. Spry, in which all three attempted to not quite accuse the servants of having allowed some unknown person to infiltrate the Court's grounds for an unspecified nefarious purpose, whilst simultaneously deriding the staff for thinking anything untoward had happened at all.

After which, he had been visited by his sister Nan, who was in a rare state of agitation. It was an agitation he began to share, when taken together with Jack's decidedly odd behavior of the night before, and while he was at pains to convince Nan that she was worrying over a nothingness, he was now faced with the prospect of finding a way to get himself out of the Court without anyone else being the wiser.

It would have to be after the household was asleep, of course, and that raised the problem of those confounded hounds. Peterkin was not, however, much troubled by that. They might be foul, vicious beasts, but they were still dogs, when all was said and done, and Peterkin knew a thing or two about dogs. Still, were anyone to find him where he should not be...

He managed to slip unnoticed into the cool-room, where the remains of the previous night's meats were kept, and to purloin two nearly-intact shanks of beef. These and his mother's specially-brewed Valerian Tincture were all he needed to make his midnight departure quiet enough, he reckoned, so long as the ostler's boy he was sharing a room over the stables with did not decide to have a wakeful night.

"THESE DREADFUL GLYPHS," the author of "*Ancient Alchemies*" had written, "*are fortunately so extremely Rare, and so difficult to utilize, that very few instances of their harmful and dangerous Influences are known. Only*

the strongest and most knowledgeable may even think of handling them, for their evil Charms and malevolent Properties will oftentimes recoil back upon their wielders, causing great mayhem, while refusing to perform as required.

"And it is for these reasons that those with Higher Powers are most intently scrutinized and examined for moral probity, and for strong Bindings to be laid upon them, so that they shall not be tempted into Transgression.

"Still, 'tis wise for others to know and recognize the chiefest ones, so that they do not fall into the hands of the unwary or the unscrupulous, but delivered to the Authorities for destruction.

"The iniquities of these Glyphs are never so apparent as when they come into close contact with objects of an opposite nature. For example, an Emblem of Purity, such as a Spring Rose, will easily succumb to any sort of Glyph of Absorption, for these objects will attempt to Assimilate the Life Forces they are exposed to, even without the Ritual of Binding. The rose will appear to die a most dreadful demise, yet remain also living, in a curious way, imitating the Glyph's intended purpose, which is to effect a kind of link whereby the Glyph may transfer the Victim's Life and Will to another."

The book slipped from Polly's trembling hands.

IN THE DRAWING ROOM, Eglantine had sunk down onto a velvet-covered chaise, her hand at her temple.

"I fear I have the most dreadful head--ache coming on," she said.

"I expect it will rain tonight," Lady Mayland said, faintly. "I always have a megrim when it is going to rain. You father has often remarked upon it."

"Tea will soon set you to rights," Mrs. Anwing said.

"Oh, drat the tea," Cousin Albertine muttered. "The poor girl should be abed."

"Perhaps," Mrs. Anwing said, as if inspired, "Perhaps some lemon cordial would do better tonight. It is most soothing to the nerves." She rang the bell.

UPSTAIRS, Nan had turned back the embroidered coverlet on Miss Polly's bed and was laying out the cambric nightdress.

For a few hours, her brother's prosaic opinion that she was a pea-goose and a noddy-head – why on earth should it distress her that the master of the house was fretting for his guests' safety? – had calmed her spirits, but as the evening had fallen, her worries returned. There had been a look in his lordship's eyes that did not speak of concern.

Peterkin had not seemed to think there was anything odd in a blackened rose petal, but suddenly it occurred to her that he had been mighty careful to take it up and stow it in a pocket, instead of discarding it as the inconsequential rubbish he had so forcefully told her it was.

She sat down on the window seat, determined to wait for her young lady, rather than returning to the servant's hall to while away the time until she was needed. Indeed, the thought of spending an hour or two listening to the idle gossip from the scullery girls, or watching the second parlour-maid and the third footman flirting with each other in a way her mam would have called bold as brass and not what any good girl would allow, seemed impossible.

POLLY'S RETURN to the drawing room coincided, not unexpectedly, with the flurry of activity that always accompanied the end of an evening at Valremer Court, as the ladies retrieved their fans and handkerchiefs, and made their courtesies to their hostess.

It was not that she had lingered in the library for that purpose, although that had, perhaps, been her desire when she had first made her excuses. The confirmation of her suspicions about the token the late duke had given her had not even been the worst of it, for as she had read on, her horror had grown. The various purposes and uses of the artefacts, rituals, and concoctions the author described were uniformly so destructive and malignant, she could scarcely credit her own eyes.

But the truth of it was plain to see.

It had, perforce, taken her more than a little time to compose herself, and to overcome her fears enough to think at all; and then, when she had made and discarded six or seven plans that might convince her aunt and uncle to quit this place, it dawned on her that only the truth might serve. If she could hold these dark forces at bay until her uncle returned, and she could show him the decaying rose...

Polly pulled a random volume of "The Histories" from its place, and walked slowly back to the drawing room, just in time to voice her good-nights, and to follow in Cousin Albertine's wake up the stairs.

CAPTAIN AUSTIN DID NOT APPEAR in the private parlour of the Golden Sun that evening.

He sent no message, and Andrew, having waited nervously until well past the first set of Evening Bells, dined alone. It was a relief, but he suspected only a temporary one, since this absence seemed to him to be an indication that he was now a suspected party, and not to be trusted.

After sunset, he strolled out into the tap-room, unable to bear any longer the dire possibilities his changed status might bring. It was all very well for Major Everard to say his co-operation here would improve his status in the Army, but Andrew was under no illusions about what damage a few well-chosen words on the Captain's part could do to his career.

There were a couple of troopers from the little band of Excise men in a corner, but he ignored them, and they seemed all too happy to return that favour. Instead, he found a bench as far from them as he was able, and ordered a tankard of ale.

He was still sitting there when the last of the Evening Bells rang out, and the troopers departed.

His tankard sat untouched. Even the ale had not been enough to distract his worried thoughts, and not long after, he rose and went out into the streets.

He had no plan. His missives to the major had garnered no replies, and it suddenly occurred to him that he had no real assurance that the entire thing was not some enormous trick. Why this should be so, and how the man from the holly-hedges could have become involved escaped him, but his doubts had begun to multiply, and he could see no way out of the mess he very much feared he was in.

"Sir."

The voice was soft, nearly a whisper.

"Young sir, please."

Andrew turned and looked into the shadows of the little alley that ran behind the Golden Sun.

"Sir, there's doings up at t'Court. Evil doings."

"What? What do you mean?"

"Mad Jack said...he said if there's aught amiss, ye'd be a one who needs to know." The shadowed figure moved deeper into the gloom. "I'm off to get him word now, but ye've been told."

19

P olly could hardly bear to stay still. She had sat down at the dressing-table to let Nan brush her hair, but it was all she could do not to leap up and rush out into Eglantine's room to pour out her terrors.

But she needed to be calm, she told herself. Just a little longer, and Nan would be gone, and she could find a better hiding place for her father's book. She could hold out, then, until her uncle returned and she could unburden herself. He would understand, once she showed him the rose. He must.

"Miss?"

Polly looked at Nan's reflection in the mirror. There was a deep crease to the young woman's forehead, and her eyes were filled with...fear?

"What is it?" Some tiff in the servants' hall, no doubt. Why the girl should think she could do anything about it was a mystery, but Polly, always softhearted, tried to assume an air of concern.

"I don't wish to speak out of turn, truly, I don't, miss. But this afternoon..." Nan faltered, then said in a rush, "The master, miss. He was here. He never did such a thing before, not to anyone, not that he's had so many guests before, but still...and after, I noticed some things been disarranged, like, and miss, I don't like it, and I thought you should know!"

Polly's heart began to thump.

"Disarranged?" She pulled away from Nan and scrambled off the cushioned chair, panicking.

"Your things, miss. In the wardro-,"

But Polly was already leaping across the room and pulling at the armoire doors. She knelt and wrenched open the drawer at the base, flinging her Meresian shawl to the floor and tumbling out her glove boxes and her jewel case after it.

The book. She clutched at it, and flipped open the pages.

The rose was gone.

Eglantine's room lay at the far end of the corridor, between the very best guest bedroom occupied by Lady Mayland, and the doorway to belowstairs.

It was curious, Polly thought, as she raced down past the bits of antique statuary that graced the hallway, that none of the lamps were lit. It was late, to be sure, but generally, she thought, the servants did not extinguish them until all the occupants on this floor were well abed...

More curious still, Eglantine's door was just slightly ajar.

Out on the road west out of Summerpoole, a fox on the hunt cowered under the bushes at the verge, as a horse's hooves thundered past.

The landlord of the Golden Sun was grumpily wiping down the empty tables, a job his son usually managed for him.

But not tonight. Tonight Young Tompkin had other fish to fry, and his parent was not at all happy about it. It was all very well for the lad to work with Old Joe and the others, on a moonless night.

Bringing in the goods was a time-honoured pastime for the owners of the Golden Sun – almost a family tradition, in fact. How else was a poor landlord to get Preserving Charms for his ale and pies? The Quality certainly had no wish to share those useful items with lesser beings.

But tonight's doings? That was quite another tale to tell. What call had Tompkin to go running off to do the bidding of someone like Peterkin, without so much as a by-your-leave? And why should Old Joe have jumped up with so much fervor over a message from an incomer – even if that incomer was as famous as Mad Jack?

But there it was. Neither of them had so much as hesitated.

And the landlord was very much afraid of what this night's doings might bring.

EVEN BEFORE SHE stepped into Eglantine's room, she had known what she would find.

An empty bed.

The coverlet was turned down, and she could see, even in the dim light from the windows, a head-shaped depression on the pillow, but otherwise, the place was quiet and undisturbed. The silence was overwhelming.

The panic, curiously, fell away from her. Her worst fears were manifest and true, incontrovertibly so, and in a strange way, this had a calming effect.

The urgency did not abate, however: she ran to her aunt's room and pounded on the door.

There was no answer, at first. Polly thumped on the wood again.

There was a faint groan from inside.

"Aunt! Aunt Mayland! Please – you must wake up!"

No answer came, but the door across the hallway opened, and she turned to see Cousin Albertine, still fully dressed, emerging with a wrathful countenance.

"Polyantha Mayland! What kind of ill-bred nonsense is th-,"

"Eglantine's gone," Polly gasped out. "It's Valremer. They mean some evil!"

There was a tiny silence.

"I knew it," Cousin Albertine said, grimly. "I knew it from the very first. The Valremers have always been a bad lot. And That Woman. Where have they taken her?"

"I don't – I don't know." But then she stopped. That temple on the hill. So forbidding and dark. Not an out-of-fashion, disused folly, after all.

She had no need to say anything. Her cousin looked at her, and nodded. "Go on, then. Rouse the servants. I'll look to your aunt."

Polly turned and ran.

LORD MAYLAND CLIMBED out of the hired carriage and onto the graveled drive at the front doors of Valremer Court with relief.

His time in the City had been more than a little frustrating. There was, for a start, the need to calm his servants, and talk Cook out of handing in her notice – a task he had very much wished his wife there for, since her easy sympathy and tears would have accomplished this with far less effort and time. Indeed, Zephanine's ability to enter into other people's emotions and thereby win them into a mood of support was as admirable and useful as it was maddening. He had never quite understood it, but he valued it, and no more so than he had this last few days, when he had been made to do without.

The glaziers had claimed overwork, and it had cost him no small sum to bribe them into doing the repairs in something approaching speed and alacrity.

On top of all this, on the return journey, his carriage had broken an axle outside of some nameless village, and he had had to kick his heels for nearly a day, waiting for it to be mended.

He longed for a glass of claret and his bed, in exactly that order, and he was not in the least amused when his gentle knock on the enormous front doors of Valremer Court met with utter silence.

He knocked again, with a little more energy, but to no avail.

Really, this was ridiculous. It was not so very late as all that. A footman should still have been in attendance, at the very least.

He pounded on the wood, this time with real force. The doors remained shut.

He could hear, now, the faint noises of some kind of tumult. Voices. Screams of anguish, in fact.

He opened the door for himself.

THE SCENE that confronted Lord Mayland inside the grand entrance of the Court was one of utter confusion.

There were, in addition to Jenkins the butler, two footmen there, one of whom was still struggling into his coat, apparently only recently roused. Jenkins himself was arguing with the other footman, who was, it seemed, too terrified to obey some incomprehensible order he had been issued.

There was also one of the maids, or so he surmised, who was weeping noisily in a corner.

And his niece was arguing across both the footmen and Mr. Jenkins, shrieking that they must go after "them", although who she was referring to was not clear.

His wife appeared at the top of the stairs, accompanied by his cousin, and both of them seemed similarly distraught, and loudly so.

Lord Mayland had had more than enough.

"Silence!"

THE DOWAGER DUCHESS of Ambridge had passed too many solitary evenings to be surprised when her son did not, yet again, appear in the dining room. Still, his absence did worry her.

He had left the City rather abruptly several days ago, promising to return on the morrow, but she had not seen or heard from him since. That, at least, was unlike him – Jarod was, in general, rather more considerate about such things. His brother had been his model, and Adrian had always been – but here, the Duchess shook her head. It would do her no good to dwell on her son's death. Everyone, from Dr. Chambard to her friend Hermina, and even her maid, had warned her that she must not allow herself to fall into the dismals, or to think upon her memories and her grief.

Her health, Dr. Chambard said, depended on it.

It was not precisely Jarod's absence that worried her, in any case. She knew what young men were apt to be like, and she had worked hard, as fond a mamma as she was, not to interfere or be over-prudish when it came to these things. Men liked their freedom.

But for weeks, it had seemed to her that he had something on his mind, beyond the problems that inheriting his brother's position had entailed. He was carrying some burden, some secret he would not share, and it was not a happy one, that much she could see.

And then, in the last few days, something had seemed to change. The worry in his eyes remained, but something else was there, too. There was a fire in them – a kind of determination, a liveliness that had been missing since he had come so sadly home. That deadened spark had returned, and something else, too.

If she had not been so very aware that he had not ventured out into society in even the slightest degree since his brother's demise, she would have said he was in love.

But that, of course, was ridiculous.

"WHERE IS LORD VALREMER?"

Lord Mayland had managed, through only a few more questions than ought to have been necessary, to gain at least a partial understanding of the situation.

In this, his niece had been less than reliable. Polly had always been, in his estimation, the most level-headed member of his family, but tonight, her wits seemed almost disordered. She had spoken of evil Charms, of wicked, occult Plots, about dead roses and dead dukes...things he might have deemed sheer nonsense, save for the fact that his cousin had added a few pithy remarks about the Valremer family history, and finally, the one undeniably salient point, which was that Eglantine was not in her bed, nor anywhere else in the house.

He repeated his question to the butler.

"The Master," said Jenkins, austerely, "Has been Called Away."

"And Mrs. Anwing?"

"I believe her to have accompanied him."

"I see. And my daughter?"

"Perhaps," said Jenkins, "perhaps she decided to take some air."

"Don't be ridiculous," Polly snapped. "They have taken her. You know they have."

The butler winced.

Lord Mayland looked up at his wife and Cousin Albertine, who was swaying a little and clutching at her heart. She looked very unwell. Beside her, Zephanine had collapsed into a heap, weeping uncontrollably.

"Albertine," he said, in his most commanding voice.

His cousin straightened up, looked at Lady Mayland, and then met his gaze.

"Right," she said, with surprising strength, and bent to put her arm around Lady Mayland's shoulders. "Go on. I'll manage. You'll bring her back, Robert. I know you will."

Lord Mayland turned back to Polly, to ask her where exactly she thought Eglantine might be, but saw instead the open doors. His niece was gone.

⁓

ANDREW HAD EXPECTED to have to repeat his crawl through the hedges once more. It was very late, and surely, whether the figure in the shadows had been telling a true tale or not, the gates to Valremer Court would be locked by now.

It was with considerable surprise, then, as he rounded the last bend in the road, that he saw those gates still wide open, as if expecting him.

He had also, at the back of his mind, assumed he would have to contend with those huge, black hounds that had been so eagerly on the hunt on his recent visit, and he keenly regretted having rushed off without even bothering to arm himself in any way. His dress-sword was merely ceremonial, of course. Still, it might have come in handy.

But the grounds lay quiet as he rode slowly down the graveled drive. He could see, although he was less than halfway to the house, that the Court's front doors were wide open. Light shone out onto the carved stone portico.

He had no notion of what, precisely, he was going to do once he reached the place, and this, finally, did give him pause. He reined in his horse, and stopped to consider what he could possibly say that would not get him tossed out on his ear, or worse.

It was then, as he stared at those open doors, attempting to come up with some kind of reason why he should be calling on Lord Valremer so long past Late Bells, that the light from the doors flickered a little, and he saw the vague shape of a woman, racing down the steps and out across the grass, heading for the gardens.

She disappeared around the side of the Court, and Andrew, without any thought at all, turned his horse's head and followed her.

SHE WAS HALFWAY DOWN the Long Walk, and the temple stood out like a malevolent beacon already, glowing with a sickly, greenish light.

It was almost a relief, because until she saw it, Polly had not been perfectly sure that she had been right in her assumptions.

But even as her pace quickened and she reached the base of the hill, that relief was replaced by something else.

Something darker. A kind of force swept over her like a miasma of terror, and her steps slowed. Place-cursing had not been on the schoolroom curriculum, but Polly's voracious reading habits had touched on some odd topics. To be sure, they had not interested her very much, but they appeared to have left their mark, because she recognized this feeling for what it was, and remembered that one of the few remedies against such things was a Great Spell of Dispersal.

Unfortunately, that had not been something the governess had imparted to her two charges, either.

Her feet faltered and slowed even more, and reluctantly, she stopped moving at all.

And then she heard the baying of the hounds.

JOE WASN'T MUCH on hurrying. "The tides come in when they come in – ye can't rush 'em" had always been his motto.

But here he was, nonetheless, racing down the backstreets of Summerpoole in the dead of night, and he was none too pleased about it.

Still, as Peterkin said, there was little choice but to do whatever Jack said, or else they'd all be in the soup. If Valremer now knew that the glyph had arrived months ago, and that the young gentleman had snatched it out from under his lordship's nose and sworn them all to silence to boot, well, there was nothing for it but to throw their lot completely in with Mad Jack. If he couldn't get them out of this fix, no one could.

Not but what he wasn't sure they weren't goners either way. There had always been something about this that had stunk like week-old fish, and now, having seen what Jack truly was, he could well imagine that his days of midnight "fishing trips" and easy money were over.

The devil take the Quality and all their ways.

20

I f Lord Valremer and his cousin had enjoyed the fear that the existence of the slavering hounds had engendered in their guests, they might have regretted that momentary pleasure now, had they known of its consequence.

The terror of the mere thought of them lent Polly the strength she needed. She bent her entire will to one object – to reach the temple - and for a wonder, she found herself moving once more. There was a tiny moment of intense vertigo and she felt suddenly cold all over, before she was suddenly moving forward again.

She stumbled up the uneven terrain of the hill, and then further, throwing herself through the crumbling remains of a gateway, and tripping over the shallow steps of the portico to land, inelegantly, beside the marble columns of the open doorway.

There was chanting. There was the acidic, overpowering reek of sulphur, and there was thick greenish smoke rising from an iron brazier that stood in the centre of the stone cell of the folly. Just beyond that, there was the figure of Captain Austin in a dark robe, kneeling on the floor and drawing some kind of shape with a bit of chalk.

Valremer stood at the farthest end of the room, likewise in a dark-coloured robe, with the hood thrown back, a gleaming silver knife in his hands. Beside him, she saw Mrs. Anwing, holding a golden bowl.

Just a few feet in front of them, there was a black granite altar, upon which lay the unmoving body of a young woman in a white cambric nightdress.

And on her breast, there lay a glistening black rose.

~

ANDREW HAD NOT QUITE CAUGHT up to the figure he was chasing when she veered off the graveled walk and began to head up a little hill toward what he took to be a kind of old-fashioned summerhouse, done up as a picturesque ruin.

He had called out to her, but she didn't seem to hear him, and that was no great wonder: he, too, heard the sound of the dogs, howling in the night.

She had stopped, just for a moment, as if compelled by some unseen force, but before he could reach her side, she had, just as suddenly, surged forward in a great rush, and disappeared into the building.

He looked back to see the dogs, racing across the grounds, and urged his horse to greater speed.

Two strides later, the beast stopped, so precipitately that Andrew was nearly unseated, and he felt a wave of nausea flood over him.

The barking grew louder.

~

CAPTAIN AUSTIN, drawing his arcane sigil on the slate-flagged floor, did not look up, intent upon his task.

Valremer, on the other hand, did stop, mid-syllable, to look down at Polly, who had gotten to her feet. Eglantine still lay before them, motionless on the stone table.

"Miss Polyantha," he drawled, his voice heavy with amusement. "How good of you to join us."

"Murderer!" But even as she shrieked the word, Polly saw just the faintest movement on the altar. Eglantine still breathed.

Valremer turned to Mrs. Anwing. "Take her. Bind her. Let her enjoy the spectacle."

Polly barely recognized the fashionable woman that she had thought she'd known. The woman advancing on her was not the smooth-faced, gracious hostess that had been at pains to make her guests feel at ease, or even the sharp-tongued gossip that the Maylands had seen glimpses of at odd moments during their time in the City.

This woman advanced toward her with such a twisted grimace of unholy glee that Polly, already in the grip of overwhelming fear and denial, felt her heart quail. She was assailed with the sudden desire to turn and run, but even that was a half-hearted sensation, for her feet, she felt certain, would not have obeyed her in any case.

There was no time to even think, for suddenly, Mrs. Anwing was upon her and clutching at her wrist.

Polly found her feet could move, after all. She pulled away from that grasping hand, ducked, and pushed past her adversary, past the smoking iron brazier, and past the still-kneeling Captain Austin, determinedly drawing his complicated sigil on the floor.

If only she could reach Eglantine in time. Surely that would be enough to end this nightmare.

A hand seized her shoulder and wrenched her back.

IN ALL HER days in the schoolroom, no one had ever suggested that a young lady in Polyantha Mayland's position in society should ever learn to defend herself from a physical attack.

How to counter an ill-natured remark, how to react to a snub, how to depress some inferior's pretensions – those were all the weapons she had ever been supposed to have needed in life.

But desperation, Polly discovered, was just as useful a teacher as her governess had been. She turned with the force pulling at her and delivered an open-handed slap squarely into Mrs. Anwing's still grinning face.

Mrs. Anwing screamed with rage, but Polly was already on the move again.

Three more steps. Two.

She stretched out her hand, reaching for Eglantine's, but even as she touched her cousin's cold, cold skin, her adversary was on her once more, and gripping her with a strength and ferocity Polly would not have believed possible. In an instant, she had been yanked back and around to face the woman, unable to break free.

It was then that Polly saw that the man who had been working so intently on his task with the chalk was finally done, and was on his feet, looking toward the open doors.

And just past him, over the Anwing's black-robed shoulder, she saw something more. Lieutenant Calthorpe plunged precipitately into the room.

～

ANDREW WOULD NOT HAVE EVER ADMITTED to fear. In later days, he modestly allowed that the sight of the ravenous hounds had "given him pause", but this was, he said, only a momentary lapse.

In truth, he had, when a backward glance showed him that those hounds were already more than halfway across the greensward, dug his heels so fiercely into the horse's flanks that it overrode every instinct the animal might have had. Prince had reared up, leaping ahead, and was nearly to the top of the rise when sense reasserted itself, and they came to an unexpected halt.

But when Andrew twisted in the saddle to see what doom awaited him, he saw that the dogs, far from following, were stymied. They jumped and quivered, but whatever occultish force had stopped the horse when it had reached the hill was having the same effect on them: they strained and yelped, but seemed unable to go further.

Andrew slithered down from the horse's back, and ran up the

steps, only to meet, to his eternal shock, someone he would not, before this moment, have truly believed he would see.

∾

THE RELIEF that Polly's face must have shown at the sight of a friend did not deter Mrs. Anwing in the slightest. She raised a clenched fist in a most unladylike fashion.

"You little witch," Mrs. Anwing said. "I'm going to enjoy this."

"Harridan," Polly gasped, and threw herself sideways as hard as she could.

Mrs. Anwing, her arm already in mid-swing, overbalanced, let go of her victim, and fell, face first, onto the slate flagging, with a sickening thump.

Valremer howled in fury, and raised the silver knife.

∾

"HALT!" Captain Austin yelled.

The Army had done its best with Andrew. The training, however, was not as efficacious as they liked to think. Orders might be orders, but tonight, Andrew was having none of it.

He looked at his commanding officer for a brief second, and then, without any real thought at all, planted what anyone who knew him would have called an uncharacteristically scientific facer.

Austin dropped to the ground with a most gratifying speed.

∾

EGLANTINE! She must get to her – that was Polly's only thought, now.

She turned back to the altar, horrified to see that Valremer had grabbed her cousin's unresisting hands and was dragging her from the stone table.

Polly started to move, but before she had taken the first step, something gripped her ankle and she found herself tumbling down.

"I'll pay you back, you stupid girl!" Mrs. Anwing hissed.

There was, at that very moment, an unearthly crash of thunder. The columns shook, and bits of plaster and dust from the frescoed ceiling pattered down onto Polly's head.

And just for an instant, everything stopped. Even the dogs outside were silenced.

In the doorway, haloed by green-tinged moonlight, there stood a tall, muscular man in a woolen greatcoat, holding a still-smoking blunderbuss, and looking distinctly unimpressed.

The rafters creaked.

Lord Valremer pushed Eglantine back onto the altar, and his mouth twisted.

"*You!*"

The man in the doorway laughed.

LORD MAYLAND HAD NOT THOUGHT he had hesitated for more than a few moments before going after his niece, but once outside, he could see nothing of her.

What he did see was a party of three men, running down the drive and then turning off toward the west side into the gardens.

It occurred to him that the men might not have anything to do with his daughter's disappearance, but having no other option, he set off in pursuit.

A fool's errand, he thought, moments later, and dangerous, too, for he could hear the sound of dogs barking, and belatedly remembered those fearsome hounds that had so upset the Females of his family.

The men seemed to have no such qualms. Indeed, the beasts seemed to be their especial object, for, as they entered the Long Walk, they did not slow, but set an even faster pace, until Lord Mayland despaired of keeping them in sight, let alone catching up to them.

It was at that point that he saw their goal.

The folly, as he and Polly had supposed it to be, stood out in stark silhouette at the top of a small rise above the lake. An unearthly, greenish smoke was drifting from the entrance, and at the base of the hill, Valremer's dogs were barking madly and lunging at some unseen barrier.

Just then, he heard a horse's hooves pounding across the lawn, and saw a blur of motion as a single rider galloped past him, past the men Lord Mayland had been following, and past the dogs, too.

Whatever held those creatures at bay had no effect on the rider. His horse leapt over the pack and up the hill, where the man slid out of the saddle, ran to the doorway, and was inside before Lord Mayland could even think to call out to him.

There was a muffled boom from inside the folly, and the whole edifice seemed to shake. Lord Mayland's dread reached panic levels. He began to run faster.

The men, on the other hand, had stopped, yards away from the dogs. One of them put his hand to his lips, and an instant later, the dogs turned, tails flat and tongues suddenly silent. Then they skulked, unwillingly, back to the Walk, where they grouped together, milling around the men, and whining piteously as they meekly allowed themselves to be leashed.

"Here, hold up, sir," one of them cried out as Lord Mayland came closer. "Best hold up, sir, an' let Jack handle it!"

He paused, if only to catch his breath. "You don't understand," he said. "My daughter, she's –,"

"Oh, we know, right enough," said the oldest of the men. "Beggin' yer lordship's pardon, but we know more'n you, I warrant. But you'd best stay back. Jack don't need no interferences, he says, and I believe him."

MRS. ANWING LET GO of Polly, and staggered to her feet.

At a nod from her cousin, she raised her hands, crooking her fingers.

"Gudanna Alani!"

A red fork of lightning arched out from her fingertips, straight toward the door.

The man did not move.

The lightning crackled against a sudden flare of blue light, inches away from his face.

And then he began to walk, slowly, deliberately, down the length of the room.

Valremer frowned, and reached for his victim again, only to look down in dismay.

Eglantine had slid from the altar, and was crouching on the farther side of the stone, out of reach.

And the rose? It lay on the slate flagging beside her, and among the decaying petals, there lay a small disc of twisted, coiled black stone that seemed to pulse and twist in the flickering light.

Valremer's expression tightened.

The man was only a few feet away.

His lordship raised the knife again and pointed it towards the newcomer.

"Emuqu Nekella!"

The fire in the brazier flared up, deeply green, and the flames leapt out like some enormous hammer.

The force hit the man in the greatcoat squarely in the back.

He staggered, and then dropped to his knees.

"Jack!"

Polly could have wept with despair.

Valremer smiled. He walked calmly around to stand looking down at the man, and after a moment, stretched out his arms.

Polly's arms were outstretched, too. She clenched her eyes shut and said the only words she could remember at all.

"Isatri Igisum!"

Master Sempervirens would not have been at all impressed.

21

The fireworks that erupted were not even the half-hearted bouquets that she had managed during her lessons. They resembled nothing in nature, and, not having formed even the vaguest picture in her mind before releasing the spell, the explosion was a mass of every colour imaginable, brilliant with all the rage and despair that had been building in Polly's breast for the last hour and more.

And just this once, it had manifested precisely where she wanted it to: less than an inch in front of Valremer's nose.

His lordship dropped the knife and staggered back, his hands to his face.

THE MAN CALLED Mad Jack had indeed told his henchmen not to interfere, come what might, but that had been hours ago, and he might have disagreed with his own advice at that moment, for the fireworks had not slowed his adversary down for long.

The explosion had spent most of its force on Valremer, to be sure, but Jack had not escaped unscathed. For several long moments, he, too, had been blinded by the burst of colour and fire that had suddenly manifested above him, and although he had recovered more quickly, his opponent was not as seriously injured as one might have hoped.

Indeed, just as he got to his feet, his eyes still a little dazzled by the glare of the explosion, Jarod saw that his problems were far from over. Valremer, too, was struggling to rise, his face blackened with smoky residue, and he was groping blindly for the knife.

He advanced on his lordship, intending to end this once and for all, when he heard Polly's scream of frustration, and turned.

Mrs. Anwing had not been deterred by the apparent defeat of her cousin's aims. She had used the distraction of the fireworks to advantage, and flung her arms around Polly from behind, rendering that young lady powerless to do anything but struggle uselessly.

He heard Valremer's movement, just an instant before he felt the man's arm wrap itself around his neck and begin to tighten.

He jabbed his elbow back into Valremer's midsection, hard, but there was no reaction. Or rather, there was, but not the one he'd hoped for: the arm around his neck tightened even more, and he felt his airways beginning to close.

Jack planted his feet onto the ground as hard as he could, and with all the strength he had left, heaved himself backward.

They tumbled through the air, and, as they hit the ground, he felt the arm around his neck slacken in its grip, and he pushed against it, gasping.

He managed, a moment later, to roll away and onto his knees. Valremer was wheezing for breath too, but obviously was not finished yet, for he began to push himself up, a feral violence in his eyes.

Jack managed to get to his feet.

This was no time for niceties, or for the gentlemanly rules of fisticuffs.

POLLY HAD WATCHED the two men grapple, even as she tried vainly to free herself from Mrs. Anwing's grasp. She heard the woman begin to laugh when Valremer had clamped his arm around Jack's neck, and at that, for a brief instant, she knew real despair, for it seemed to her that all hope must now be lost.

But at that very moment, she heard a grunt of surprise, and the Anwing's hands released her.

And then Jack got up, and without even the slightest hesitation, kicked Valremer squarely in the chest.

ANDREW HAD VIEWED THE SCENE, as it unfolded, with considerable horror.

He had been just a touch worried, after he'd vanquished the captain, that he might have gotten this all wrong, but the sight of Valremer laying his hands on Eglantine's obviously ensorcelled body, with equally obvious malicious intent, had assured him that he was on the right side of this imbroglio.

His only object, now, was to rescue Eglantine. As soon as Mad Jack had arrived, Andrew had gotten on the move, slipping carefully along the shadows of the west wall, with the sole mission of retrieving Eglantine and carrying her to safety.

But then all those confounded spells had begun to go off, and he saw that things were in no wise so certain. The man in the greatcoat had been – well, not bested, not yet, but certainly in a bad case.

Jack had let go of the blunderbuss when Valremer had played his scurvy trick of Force hitting from behind. The weapon now lay only a few feet from Andrew's toes.

He picked it up, unsure of what to do. It was certainly heavy – all the common soldiers he knew complained about the weight.

He couldn't re-load it. He hadn't anything to load it with. Still...

One should never hit a Female, of course. But then, one was also supposed to render a lady every assistance possible.

He swung the blunderbuss in a nice, wide arc, and made sure that Mrs. Anwing, at least, would have no further part in this night's work.

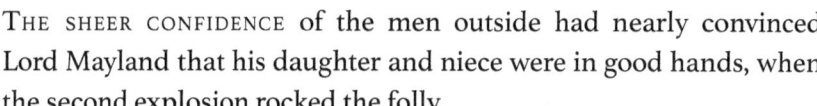

THE SHEER CONFIDENCE of the men outside had nearly convinced Lord Mayland that his daughter and niece were in good hands, when the second explosion rocked the folly.

This time, he did not stop to heed their pleas, but began running, once again, towards the source of his fears.

At the base of the hill, whatever had stopped those dogs from achieving their goal stopped him as well.

Like Polly, he knew at once what it was.

Unlike his niece, he needed no overpowering or desperate fear to overcome it. It might have been two full decades and more since he had attended lectures at the Academy, but Lord Mayland had never neglected his sparring sessions with old Sempervirens and other Practitioners, and Great Spells were still at his disposal. He uttered a single word of Power, and felt a trembling in the air, as the curse wavered, and he stepped easily into the gap he'd opened.

LORD MAYLAND MOVED through the open doorway, only to stop just over the threshold to survey the scene with some anxiety.

There were three bodies, for a start, and while he had no way to know, just yet, whether they were dead or alive, it seemed likely that none of them were persons whose demise would seriously trouble him. On the other hand, he was fairly sure that the authorities might disagree.

He saw one of Eglantine's admirers was there, still holding a heavy firearm as if it were a club, and with a certain martial gleam in his eye. Lieutenant Calthorpe had never impressed Lord Mayland as anything but a useless fribble before, but at the sight of him now, he began to revise his opinion.

His niece was standing alone, and her attention was fixed upon the final occupant of the room - a rather disreputable-looking man clad a coat of the most unfashionable kind. It could not be said that the man was insensible of Polly's regard, either – indeed, he seemed almost enthralled by her gaze.

"Polly?" said the man, eventually. "Polly, are you hurt?"

"I? No, no. But, Jack..." she broke off, for she saw that Eglantine was still huddled against the side of the altar, and apparently was aware of only one other person in that place.

"Andrew," she cried. "Oh, Andrew, take me away from here!"

The Lieutenant did not hesitate. In a trice, he had closed the distance and gathered Eglantine into his arms.

Lord Mayland said her name, very loudly.

"Oh!" said his daughter, looking up. She blushed, but did not make the slightest attempt to remove herself from Andrew's embrace.

Lord Mayland sighed inwardly. Zephanine, he had no doubt, would enact a tragedy over this, and what his sharp-tongued cousin was likely to say would very probably be worse, but he knew defeat when it stared him in the face.

"Lieutenant, if you would be so good as to take my daughter back to the house...?"

Lord Mayland watched them go, satisfied that his future son-in-law looked properly grateful for the trust reposed in him. Then he turned his attention back to the more serious problem at hand.

He looked at the blackened rose on the floor, and at the blackened stone at its centre, and nodded, grimly.

He looked to the three bodies on the floor, and the man in the greatcoat.

"Are they dead?"

"Valremer is. And his cousin, too, I think. Calthorpe don't know his own strength, I reckon."

It was so quiet, now. Polly could hear her own breathing.

"Well," said Lord Mayland, after a long moment. "What's to be done about all this? It will be devilish hard to explain it, even with that – that thing there."

"Well, as to that," said Jack, "I think you are the most proper person to arrange it. And I'll thank you if you could leave me out of it, m'lord."

"Jack!" Polly found herself outraged. "Jack, you cannot mean it! If you had not come when you did..." She shuddered.

"My niece has the right of it," Lord Mayland said. "It seems to me that the credit is all yours. You saved my daughter and my niece – and perhaps many others."

"Not without the Lieutenant's help. And yourself, sir."

"I? I did nothing."

"That's not what the world will like to know."

"But surely – your part in it ought to be recognized?"

"Nay. No one would believe it, in any case."

"Jack," Polly could not contain herself any longer. "Jack, you ought not say so! It was you, all of it, and the world should know it!"

He shook his head. "Your uncle knows I speak the truth. It's for the best, love. Truly, it is."

Lord Mayland looked at him, very hard.

"I know you, do I not?" he said.

"I shouldn't think so, m'lord."

Lord Mayland opened his mouth, and then shut it, very firmly. There was a long silence.

"As you wish," Lord Mayland said, quietly.

"It's for the best, sir. For me and for her."

"Perhaps you are right," Lord Mayland said, abruptly. "Just as you like, then. The credit can go to young Calthorpe."

"And his commanding officer," Jack said. "A Major Everard, I believe. I feel sure they will corroborate any details of the thing, if you ask them to."

"Ah. That sounds likely," Lord Mayland agreed. He looked at his niece. "Best that you and I return to the house, Polly. You aunt will want to see you are unharmed."

"Oh," Polly whispered. "Oh, please..."

Jack coughed, discreetly.

"If I might have, m'lord, just a moment?"

Lord Mayland hesitated, then nodded. "Polly, I will wait outside for you. But do not be long"

"POLLY."

Tears stung her eyes.

"Polly, m'love. Do not weep. It's all over. You're safe now."

"That's not why I..."

"I know." Jack had taken her hands in his. "I know. But you must forget this horror. You must."

"I – I cannot!"

She looked up at him. He was smiling, just a little, ruefully, and it came to her that she had seen a smile like that before, although she could not think of just where or when.

And then he let her go, and turned away.

22

I n the City, the weather had finally broken. Chilly winds blew
down the avenues and alleys, and a new style of short-waisted
jacket with enchanted buttons became the rage for every lady.

Eglantine's reappearance was heralded as the best event of the
Season, and her engagement announcement as an occasion of utter
bliss. Indeed, many a less-favoured young woman of fashion seemed
overjoyed at the news, and offered heartfelt congratulations.

Whatever misgivings her mother or Cousin Albertine might have
harboured were set to rest when Andrew's part in unraveling the
nefarious doings on Valremer's estate became known, for in addition
to his being decorated for courage, Andrew had become a figure of
both renown and romance.

This was furthered by respect for Andrew's own demeanor. He
steadfastedly refused the appellation of "hero", preferring to
modestly showcase the role of others, even including the stalwart
assistance of the men of Summerpoole's backstreets, and only
allowing that he'd done what any gentleman would have felt
compelled to do under the circumstances: that when a man saw evil
and wickedness, he acted to correct it, and defend the Right and
the Good.

It was universally agreed that Eglantine was quite the lucky young lady, but that she deserved her good fortune.

IN THE WEEKS that followed their return, Polly found she could not quite understand herself.

She was certainly quite wholeheartedly happy for Eglantine. She felt sure that her cousin's marriage would be everything delightful that could be imagined, since Andrew's sole object in life seemed now to be to create a future of calm and happiness for his betrothed, even to the point of resigning his commission.

Eglantine, to be sure, had loyally declared herself positively enchanted by the prospect of following the drum, as it were, but Andrew's uncle had joined forces with Cousin Albertine. Together, they had convinced the young lovers that they would do far better to engage a townhouse each Season, and spend the bulk of their days at Calthorpe Hall, learning the business of estate and household management. This, combined with the generous allowance Cornelius Calthorpe declared would be theirs if they chose that route, had made Andrew's decision an easy one.

She was glad for them both. She was not even the tiniest bit jealous. She was truly and unabashedly happy for her cousin.

She ought to be happy for herself.

She had every reason to be: her own return to the City had been greeted with nearly as much enthusiasm as her cousin's had been. Despite every one of Eglantine's other suitors having had to give up their hopes, Polly found she still did not lack for dance partners, and they continued to jostle for the right to hand her into the carriage at the end of the night.

Eglantine had not been mistaken: she was liked for her own sake.

The invites had continued to pour in, and the entertainments offered were as varied and inventive as they had always been.

So why was she not content?

Why did she continue to look up and down Shalliton Place, every time she walked out the doors?

Why did the sight of any common street vendor in a woolen coat make her hear skip a beat?

Why did she feel, in her moments alone, this hollowness in her heart?

She was a fool. She knew it. He was a rogue and a scoundrel, and he had known, they both had known, there was nothing in it for either of them. She must put him out of her mind.

THE INVITATION ARRIVED on a morning like any other. Eglantine, having swallowed a half piece of toast and two gulps of tea, had rushed off to Honorine's for her final fitting of the delicately embroidered silver gown she had chosen to be wed in, Lord Mayland had left for his club, declaring himself useless for anything other than meeting the staggering collection of bills that were mounting up, and Lady Mayland was sorting through the vast pile of correspondence that the Post had yielded up for her.

"Oh!" she said, suddenly. "Oh, Polly, my love, I am *so* sorry! Banks must have gotten this muddled – else I would never have opened your post – but, only think how grand this is!"

She held out a cream-coloured square of paper with gilt edging, and an equally handsome envelope surmounted with a wax seal.

Polly looked at the proffered missive. The Ambridge coat of arms stood out clearly on the bright red blob that had secured the envelope.

"Indeed," she said, hollowly. "There must be some mistake."

"Oh, no – the address is quite clear. And she wishes that – well, you must read it yourself!"

Polly took the letter in her hand. The Duchess had only written a few lines, in a clear and firm script, begging her, if she was not too overset with wedding preparations for her cousin, to join Her Grace for tea that afternoon.

"I don't understand. What should a duchess want with me?"

"She must be quite bored," said Lady Mayland. "All alone in that great house, with so little to amuse one. I expect I would go mad. And did you not say that she was so affable, when you met her at Lady Sackler's concert? Depend on it, it is exactly as she says: she longs for company."

She would be the last person to provide anyone with real cheer or distraction, did the duchess but know it, Polly thought, but she could not refuse. She quite saw that. If nothing else, her aunt would be distraught.

Consequently, just after the noon meal, she found herself in the foyer of the Mayland house, attired in her newest walking dress, with its matching jacket ready to button itself up against the autumn breeze outside, and waiting for the carriage the duchess had said she would be only too delighted to send, *"for I expect all the resources one's family has are otherwise occupied, as they should be, for the forthcoming happy occasion!"*

Her mood was reluctant still. It had occurred to her that some faint rumour of her late son's brief attention to the Mayland poor relation might have come to Her Grace's ears, and that the lady might be under the impression that Polly would perhaps have had some lingering tenderness over this. With her thoughts so far from that evening, and her heart so otherwise distracted, she was, she concluded, possibly the worst person the duchess could have asked for in terms of shared emotions.

Polly heard the carriage wheels outside the door, and put her own melancholy aside. The lady had been kind to Polly, and concerned for her. This was probably just more of the same, and she ought to be grateful for that.

THE DRAWING ROOM Polly was ushered into was furnished in the most elegant style, and Her Grace was everything that was gracious and kind.

To Polly's relief, she seemed in no way disposed to discuss her guest's single encounter with the late duke, or even the recent demise of Lord Valremer, and all that this had exposed. There was, of course, no reason the duke's passing fancy should have come to her ears at all, Polly realized, and relaxed as the Duchess, with an indolent gesture, levitated the teapot, caused it to pour, and began to inquire about the wedding preparations.

"Of course she would look radiant in silver," Her Grace agreed, when Polly described Eglantine's dress. "She has the colouring for it. You would not suit it – gold would be the better choice for you, I think."

There was a discreet knock on the door to the drawing room, and a footman appeared.

"His Grace desires you to step into the library, if you please, ma'am."

"Oh," said the duchess. Her smile was broad. "Of course. Miss Mayland, do excuse me! I do not think I shall be but a moment."

POLLY GOT UP AND WALKED, aimlessly, to the windows.

It was raining, just a little. She could see the first droplets on the glass panes, as if even the weather wanted to weep with her.

She took hold of herself. Really, she must not do this. She must try to appear cheerful. She must, for everyone's sake, and perhaps, if she worked hard enough at it, it would someday be true.

Behind her, she heard the door open again, and turned back to her hostess.

Then she gasped, for the person that had entered the room was, most assuredly, not the Duchess of Ambridge.

She took in only that face – a face she had not thought to ever see again – with a rush of shocked joy, a joy that was swiftly replaced by consternation.

"Jack!" she said. "Jack – how can you – oh! You cannot be here! You must go, at once!"

He smiled. "I think not, my love."

It was then that she began to take it all in. He had left off the rough wool. He was now attired in an extremely fashionable tailcoat and trousers, and his hair appeared to have been recently trimmed and dressed in an artful style of disarray. The truth of it left her speechless – and suddenly furious.

"You! Oh, how could you?" She could feel the colour flooding her face, and blinked back tears of rage. "I suppose you thought it a fine joke? Well, I am not laughing, sir!"

He crossed the room in two long strides, and captured her hands in his.

"No, my love. No. I never meant – at least, once I knew - well, what I meant is of no consequence, now."

She pulled away. At least, she tried to. But her body would not obey: she found herself trembling, and a single tear slid down her cheek.

"Polly," he said, softly. "Polly, love, do not – I beg of you! If you only knew...It was just that I dared not let anything slip until we'd stopped Valremer's schemes. He drove my brother to his death, and he had to be stopped. It was the only way. Surely you must see that?"

The thing was, she did see it. She had just been a means to an end, and the fact that the end had been the same one she herself had been trying for, more or less, did not take the sting from it. She turned her face away.

"I didn't know," he said. "I didn't know what Adrian had done. He sent me a letter, explaining it, but he couldn't write out in plain terms what he'd done with the glyph. He did his best – I couldn't think why he'd quoted your father's words about the flowers of spring, you see, and then – well, he knew me better than I know myself."

"Did he? I am very well enlightened, Your Grace," Polly said, coldly. "Naturally, he had no choice but to make use of the first female he came across. It seems to be a habit in your family."

"You don't understand," he said, with desperation. "He didn't do it on a whim. Or without knowing how much risk there was for you. He said it in his letter, he warned me to get you out of it, and quickly, too, but I was such a slow-top – I nearly lost you because of my stupidity." He stopped, and let go of her hands. "There's no forgiving it. I know that. Only, Polly, please. Do not weep. I can't bear it."

She couldn't listen to him. She would not. She would stop her pounding heart, and leave aside her tears. She would walk away from this unbearable heartache.

She didn't move.

"Polly, please."

"Why should you care what I feel, Your Grace?" Her voice shook. "Why should it matter to you? The thing is done, and you can go on with your life. And I with mine."

"But that's the trouble," he said. "I can't just go on. Not without you."

Her heart began to pound harder.

Polly tilted her face up to his.

This time, his kiss did not make her in the least bit angry.

ACKNOWLEDGEMENTS

This book owes a lot to a lot of people: Jane Austen and Georgette Heyer, for a start, as well as to Nancy Moors, whose on-line writing prompt sparked the initial idea. I'm grateful to her, along with Aaron-Michael Hall, who both gave such useful feedback. Finally, to my parents, who taught me to love reading with all the fiery passion of a thousand suns, and, as always, to Pat, who believed. I miss you, sweetie.

ABOUT THE AUTHOR

Morgan Smith has been a goatherd, a landscaper, a weaver, a bookstore owner, a travel writer, and an archaeologist, and she will drop everything to travel anywhere, on the flimsiest of pretexts. Writing is something she has been doing all her life, though, one way or another, and now she thinks she might actually have something to say.

If you downloaded this book without purchase from a pirating site, please read it with the author's compliments. If you enjoy it, please consider purchasing a legal copy to support the author in writing further books. If you can't afford to buy it, please leave a review on Smashwords or Goodreads – it really helps!

ALSO BY MORGAN SMITH

Novels in the Averraine Cycle:
Casting in Stone
A Spell in the Country
The Shades of Winter

Flashbacks: an unreliable memoir of the '60s

SOCIAL MEDIA

Connect with me on social media!

Facebook: https://www.facebook.com/morgansmithauthor
Twitter: https://twitter.com/morganauthor1
Blog: https://morgansmithauthor.wordpress.com
Website:
https://theaverrainecycle.wordpress.com/2017/06/18/welcome-to-averraine/

www.ingramcontent.com/pod-product-compliance
Lightning Source LLC
Chambersburg PA
CBHW071246130626
46556CB00003B/1186